STAR WARS™
ALIEN ARCHIVE

Printed in the United States of America
First Edition, April 2019
1 3 5 7 9 10 8 6 4 2

Library of Congress Control Number on file
FAC-034274-19081
ISBN 978-1-368-02735-9

Visit the official *Star Wars* website at:
www.starwars.com.

PRESS

Los Angeles • New York

STAR WARS™
ALIEN
ARCHIVE

ILLUSTRATED BY

TIM McDONAGH

INTRODUCTION

The Graf Archive on Orchis 2 is home to a wealth of data yet undiscovered. As part of an ongoing restoration, a task force has been assembled to search the darkest corners of the vast library for lost treasures of historical importance. Led by archive droid TR-33NA, work has begun in earnest. One of our first significant finds, deep within the stacks, was an old journal full of sketches, annotations, and more than a few tall tales from a mysterious traveler.

This unknown explorer speaks of many lively locations, with stories of aliens from all over the galaxy. Accounts of battles and adventures, foreign cultures, and famous members of multiple species are annotated and illustrated by an expert hand.

Sadly, the journal has faded and become damaged over the years, meaning the true identity of its author is hard to determine. The sketches, however, do resemble the work of famed Ithorian artist Gammit Chond. Chond was rumored to have been a recluse, but his knowledge of the wider galaxy leads some historians to believe him to be a great adventurer after all. Perhaps we will never know. . . .

The traveler was fond of a fun atmosphere and often flew to wherever he was sure to meet a lot of people having a good time. We have arranged his notes according to these vibrant hubs, and the rest are organized by common landscapes, climates, and the physiologies of individual species.

Unable to authenticate the author, and therefore the accuracy of the stories within the journal, we have paired some of the content that has not been destroyed by age with data entries from our scientific records. With details of over two hundred aliens from across galactic history, we are happy to restore this enigmatic journal for public viewing.

—Xoddam Lothipp
Deputy Director, Graf Archive

DRY HABITATS

We begin by exploring the journal entries featuring those aliens who hail from, or are found in, the driest atmospheres in the galaxy. These desert dwellers make a living in hot, arid climates and adapt to sandstorms, high temperatures, and subterranean predators.

On the sand dunes of Tatooine and Jakku there are primitive people, scavengers, farmers, and herd animals all living together. On volcanic worlds, multiple species relocate and rebuild on an ever-changing landscape. Dangerous climates on Utapau and Sullust force whole societies underground.

These seemingly barren lands have hosted many important events in galactic history. The grasslands of Lothal were a key battleground in the rise of the Rebellion. The rocky caves of Jedha hid many secrets of rising resistance against the Empire. And Tatooine was home to the Skywalkers—the family of the great Force-sensitives, who changed the course of the Jedi forever.

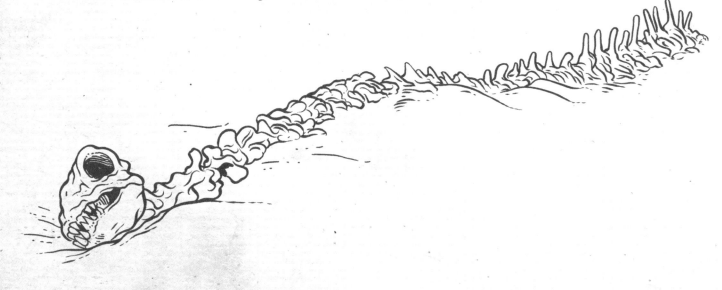

ᒐᑌᔑᑕᐯᔑᗩ 7ᖽ17ᐯ17

TUSKEN RAIDER

HOMEWORLD: TATOOINE

Tusken Raiders, also known as Sand People, are nomadic humanoids who travel in large groups and are most known for their hostility toward other settlers on Tatooine. In the harsh environment of the desert, where food is scarce, these natives become fiercely territorial and patrol the sands, attacking small settlements and stealing supplies.

WEAPONS

Each Tusken warrior creates a unique gaderffii stick, a bladed club used in combat. They are crafted out of available salvage, and each warrior becomes proficient in wielding these weapons against their enemies. The less popular weapon of the clans is the Tusken Cycler rifle. Despite their crude design, these weapons can hit targets reliably at long ranges, but the rate of fire is typically slow.

A primitive cry rang out across the dunes, scattering smaller wildlife and giving me a bit of a fright. A long line of banthas could be seen in the distance with oddly dressed travelers upon their backs. They did not look very welcoming. . . .

Traang (the curved end of a gaderffii stick): can be covered in sandbat venom, which has paralysing properties.

CULTURE

Tusken Raiders travel in clans of twenty to thirty individuals, led by a chief. Every year the fiercest young members of the tribe must prove their strength by defeating a krayt dragon and bringing home the pearl found in the dragon's stomach. The males of the species serve as warriors, protecting the tribe and attacking any trespassers on their territory. The females protect the home and raise the children. During warrior initiation rites, each individual is given a bantha matching their own gender to care for, and the pair is bonded for life.

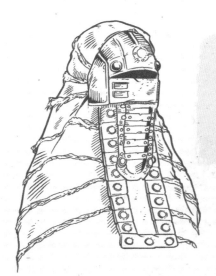

Sand People all wear plain, rough garments, but the females can be identified by elaborate jeweled masks.

Tatooine's distance from the core worlds has allowed a criminal underworld to flourish. Here I met a greedy smuggler with a horn protruding from his head.

ADVOZSE

HOMEWORLD: RIFLOR

Advozsec are a humanoid species from a volcanic planet. Their thick skin and sensitive eyes allow them to thrive in a harsh environment. On Riflor, volcanic eruptions frequently destroy Advozsec settlements, so they tend to care very little about material goods. Instead, they strive to accumulate as much monetary wealth as possible so they can continually rebuild after disaster strikes. As a species they have a very pessimistic outlook on life.

ARCONA

HOMEWORLD: CONA

Arcona are desert dwellers, easily identifiable by their unique triangular heads. They live in family-based communities and are notorious for their addiction to common salt. Hem Dazon frequently spent time in the Mos Eisley cantina after being stranded on Tatooine. He couldn't return to his home planet because he had spent all his credits on salt and juri juice.

The cantina here in Mos Eisley attracts a lot of bleak souls. One patron with a funny-shaped head tried to get me to lend him money for juri juice. . . .

ᴋᴜʙᴀᴢ (KUBAZ)

KUBAZ

HOMEWORLD: KUBINDI

Kubaz live on a diet of insects, using their long snouts to snatch their prey from inside hives. This does not make them very popular with insectile species, such as the Geonosians. They have extremely sensitive eyesight, causing them to require protective eyewear when traveling off planet. They are unable to pronounce the Basic language, speaking instead in whirring syllables.

On my way back through the Mos Eisley marketplace, I met a curious-looking Kubaz named Garindan. He wouldn't tell me much but I observed him meeting with Imperial stormtroopers, who had previously been questioning locals about the location of some missing droids. I imagine he was in their employ. . . .

While I have encountered many pleasant species, I cannot count the Pykes among them.

ᴘʏᴋᴇ (PYKE)

PYKE

HOMEWORLD: OBA DIAH

Although based on Oba Diah, the Pykes had many dealings with all the crime families on Coruscant, operating a highly profitable trade organization called the Pyke Syndicate. Most notable among this group was Lom Pyke, their leader. On Kessel, the syndicate director Quay Tolsite oversaw enslaved miners and exploited the planet's resources for profit. The Pykes on Kessel had to wear special breathing apparatus and lead-lined clothing as their poor physiology reacted badly to the harsh climate.

JAWA

HOMEWORLD: TATOOINE

Up ahead I saw a large vehicle rolling over the dunes, pulling to a halt in front of some moisture farms. The front of the vehicle opened up like a drawbridge, revealing several small creatures in dark cloaks. They proceeded to unload many droids, ship parts, and other scrap and I moved in for a closer look

Jawas are about a meter tall, are shrouded in heavy brown cloaks, and speak in a language understood by very few other species. Fewer still know what is beneath Jawa cloaks, so an air of mystery surrounds these odd creatures to this day.

CULTURE

Jawas spend their days combing the desert dunes for droids, ship parts, and scrap to sell to the locals and visiting merchants. They make a good living refurbishing what they find and haggling with moisture farmers but have a reputation for being swindlers. They are often caught selling dangerous equipment and faulty droids, but as there aren't many retail options in the desert wasteland, they usually still make the sale.

Jawas' native language, Jawaese, uses scent as well as spoken word to convey meaning, making it almost impossible to understand by outsiders. To allow them to continue their trade, Jawas communicate with their customers using a simplified version called Jawa Trade Talk.

TOOLS

The Jawas have many tools for capturing and fixing droids. Once the Jawas have a droid in their possession, they fit it with restraining bolts. They can then summon it using a Jawa droid caller. Their sandcrawlers are equipped with magnetic cranes perfect for collecting scrap from the desert floor and a suction tube that transports droids and parts to the cargo hold.

TRANSPORT

Sandcrawlers were originally used for mining on Tatooine, but Jawas use these now abandoned vehicles for transporting their wares across the desert, as well as for a mobile headquarters. These moving fortresses provide protection from the harsh climate and terrain, and their armor is strong enough to sustain attacks from many of the Jawas' adversaries.

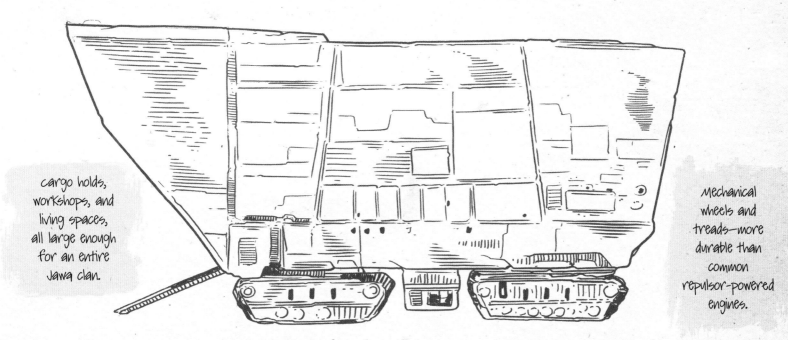

cargo holds, workshops, and living spaces, all large enough for an entire Jawa clan.

Mechanical wheels and treads—more durable than common repulsor-powered engines.

NIMBANEL

HOMEWORLD: NIMBAN

This reptilian humanoid species is famed for its problem-solving skills. They can be found demonstrating their talents throughout the galaxy, particularly in business and government. Jabba the Hutt employed a Nimbanel by the name of Mosep Binneed as one of his accountants.

I encountered an entrepreneurial air-taxi driver in Coruscant—these Nimbanels are very resourceful!

I assume Ugnaughts are technically minded, as they can often be found in engineering sectors, supplying spares for droids and even operating carbon-freezing chambers.

UGNAUGHT

HOMEWORLD: GENTES/BESPIN

This porcine humanoid species is possibly one of the hardest-working creatures in the galaxy. It's fascinating that despite originating on Gentes, many Ugnaughts now consider Bespin's Cloud City their home. According to legend, when Lord Ecclessis Figg, the well-known Corellian eccentric, struck on the idea of building a floating city, he enlisted the help of the Ugnaughts, knowing their reputation as industrious, loyal workers. In return, the Ugnaughts were given their freedom and eventually allowed to build their own home in the lower reaches of Cloud City. Sadly, many Ugnaughts who remained on Gentes were sold into slavery and are now spread throughout the galaxy.

LUTRILLIAN

HOMEWORLD: LUTRILLIA

Lutrillians tend to live a nomadic lifestyle, traveling around their homeworld and avoiding subterranean predators. They love adventure and discovery, and often travel offworld to explore other cultures. They have large, friendly faces with hairy jowls and wide-set eyes. They are considered to be very agreeable but do have a small problem with greed.

> I sat down for a game of cards with a cheerful Lutrillian, the friendliest gambler in the place.

GIVIN

HOMEWORLD: YAG'DHUL

> As much as I wanted to learn more about the Givin and his gothic appearance, I am terrible at greeting math and wanted to avoid being quizzed!

The haunting appearance of the Givin species is what most who encounter them remember. With large eye sockets and hairless heads, plus the fact that Givin walk with their arms held out in front of them, they give the impression of animated skeletons. Givin are highly intelligent and well-known for their mathematical skills. This is central to Givin society as their skills are used to monitor the climate on their home planet, to make political decisions, and to advance their engineering. Givin greet each other not with a variation of hello, but with an equation to be answered. For non-Givin, the equation comes with three possible answers. This academic prowess leads many Givin to pursue careers in scientific fields. Drusil Bephorin was a brilliant Givin cryptographer. When the Empire captured her, she worked for them in exchange for her family's safety. Bephorin was particularly skilled in probability analysis and solving complex mathematical problems, and when Luke Skywalker finally rescued her, he convinced her to lend her skills to the Rebel Alliance.

DRESSELLIAN

HOMEWORLD: DRESSEL

Dressellians are tall, bald humanoids with wrinkled skin. They lived in peaceful isolation from any conflict until the Galactic Civil War. As a species, they were loyal to the Republic, and after its demise many members joined the Rebel Alliance. Orrimaarko, a male Dressellian, was a soldier for the Alliance during the Galactic Civil War. He was part of the team that launched an assault on an Imperial shield generator during the Battle of Endor.

TOGNATH

HOMEWORLD: YAR TOGNA

These striking-looking beings are an unusual species, thanks to their insectile and mammalian characteristics. They have both an endo and exoskeleton, which gives them their unique appearance. They also possess a very primitive nervous system. While that may not sound particularly useful, it gives Tognaths the ability to be immune to most pain, which, during a time of civil war, is invaluable. This remarkable species also demonstrates basic-level telepathy between eggmates—Tognath hatchlings whose eggs grafted together before hatching. Benthic Two Tubes was a member of the Cloud-Riders, a gang led by Enfys Nest that operated during the Galactic Empire. Reunited with his brother, Edrio, the two joined Saw Gerrera's rebel cell on Jedha.

I was fascinated by the Tognath's breathing apparatus—a corrugated metal contraption, which processes oxygen on foreign planets. It only added to his menacing appearance.

IKTOTCHI

HOMEWORLD: IKTOTCH

Hailing from the harsh, wind-battered moon of Iktotch, these humanoids do not always find it easy to settle into society, despite being highly intelligent. Belying their sensitive nature, the Iktotchis' appearance, with two prolific horns growing down from either side of the head, suggests aggression, as does their tough, dark orange skin, which helps protect them against the high winds of their homeworld. They have natural telepathic and precognitive abilities, which were embraced by the Jedi but could frighten other species. The brave Jedi Saesee Tiin, renowned for his skills of telepathy, was Iktotchi.

As I traveled through the outer Rim territories my heart skipped a beat when our ship crossed paths with a band of weequay pirates. Luckily for us, they spotted a cargo freighter and set off in pursuit—a venture which no doubt proved far more profitable!

WEEQUAY

HOMEWORLD: SRILUUR

The Weequay are a humanoid species that can be commonly found throughout the galaxy. They have tough, leathery, wrinkled skin—often brown in color—which helps protect them from harsh environments (and blaster fire!), and they often keep their hair long. The Jedi Knight Que-Mars Redath-Gam was a Weequay.

ꓦ○ꓷ7ꓴꓕ

TOGRUTA

HOMEWORLD: SHILI

Togrutas are immediately recognizable by their colorful skin and long horns tipped by striped tails on their heads. They are believed to be gentle and quiet but would happily go to war for a worthy cause. This tranquil species is surprisingly skilled in combat.

All across the galaxy I encountered the beautiful colors and peaceful countenance of Togrutas. On Lothal I met Ahsoka Tano, a brave and willful Jedi warrior.

CULTURE

Togrutas originally hailed from Shili, a planet covered in colorful grasslands. The natives mirrored this vibrant scenery with distinctive patterns on their skin, which provided them with excellent camouflage. Tens of thousands of Togrutas immigrated to Kiros, building their colonies on the cliffs. Kiros is filled with beautiful green landscapes and flowing waterfalls, and Togrutas were drawn to the inspiration and tranquility this backdrop provided.

TOGRUTAS IN THE GALAXY

The most famous Togrutas were those who joined the Jedi Order. Shaak Ti was a Jedi Master and a member of the Jedi High Council. She acted as general of the Grand Army during the Clone Wars and personally oversaw the clone trooper training program. She was skilled in battle and used the Force to defeat her opponents with telekinesis.

Ahsoka Tano was another Force-sensitive Togruta, who had a heavy influence on galactic events. Ahsoka became the Padawan of Jedi Knight Anakin Skywalker during the Clone Wars. Her job was to travel with him on important missions to learn the ways of the Force. Ahsoka liked to play by the book but soon became influenced by Anakin and was later seen as reckless and hotheaded, getting involved in many sticky situations.

When she was wrongfully accused of murder and faced a trial by the Order, Ahsoka's faith in the Jedi was shaken and she decided to leave and start out on her own. Following Anakin's fall to the dark side and the destruction of the Jedi Order, Ahsoka went into hiding.

For years Ahsoka kept to the shadows, trying to avoid the Empire and helping those in need where she could. She slowly began to get involved with resistance activities, and upon meeting Senator Organa, learned of the beginnings of the Rebel Alliance. Though she preferred to work alone, Ahsoka became a key member of the organization, providing secret communications and gathering intelligence from rebel cells across the galaxy.

ᐯᑎᑌᗩᔔᗯᑌᐯ
ELNACON

HOMEWORLD: UNKNOWN

Like Gands, Elnacons hail from an ammonia-rich atmosphere and must wear special breathing apparatus when on other worlds. They are often mistaken for thugs because of their alarming height and strength but are actually a very peaceful, family-oriented species. Dava Cassamam, a deep cloud-miner on gas giant planets, was a keen sabacc player.

ᒍᛕᔔᗯᑐ
LANNIK

HOMEWORLD: LANNIK

This small humanoid species comes from a planet with a long history of war, meaning they are often brave and courageous. Their most notable feature is a pair of large, droopy ears that protrude from the head. Thanks to the size of these ears they have extremely enhanced hearing. Jedi Master Even Piell, who was mortally wounded during the Clone Wars, was a famed Lannik.

Lannik Jedi are rumored to excel in lightsaber combat. Tales of the fearsome Jedi Master Even Piell are legendary.

ᑐ1ᛞᛞᛕ7
KIFFAR

HOMEWORLD: KIFFU AND KIFFEX

The Kiffar are known for their humanlike appearance and distinguishing facial tattoos. The Jedi Master Quinlan Vos belonged to this mysterious species. He was blessed with the gift of psychometry—a talent that a small number of the species are born with. It is the gift of being able to read the memories of inanimate objects simply by touch.

I encountered a man bearing colorful facial markings. He explained that the tattoos signify the clan to which each member of the species belongs.

SWOKES SWOKES

HOMEWORLD: MAKEM TE

This little-known species has the unusual ability to regenerate body parts—particularly useful for them, as fighting is one of their natural and strongest abilities. This predisposition to violence often leads them to take positions as bodyguards and even bounty hunters throughout the galaxy. They have a reputation for being merciless ruffians caring only about themselves and vast wealth, which they see as an indication of social status. They have a particular fondness for gemstones.

where are the swokes swokes from? Their origins are a mystery despite being common sights in the galaxy—particularly around criminal enterprises where there is money to be made.

MIRIALAN

HOMEWORLD: MIRIAL

A highly spiritual group, this intelligent humanlike species is renowned for its strong connection with the natural world. They have yellow-green skin, and their faces are often covered with black geometric markings—an indication of personal achievements and expertise unique to each Mirialan. Owing to their natural belief in the Force, many Mirialans served among the Jedi, including the Jedi Master Luminara Unduli and her Padawan, Barriss Offee. It is a long-held tradition among this species that any member entering the Jedi Order must take a Mirialan as their Padawan.

TWI'LEK

HOMEWORLD: RYLOTH

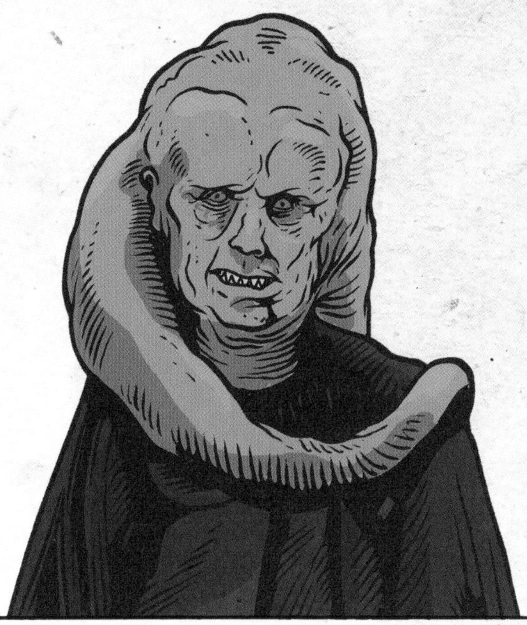

Twi'leks are a generous humanoid species prominent in many aspects of galactic life, with key players in both the Jedi Order and the resistance against the Empire. Their most noticeable feature is a long pair of tentacles called lekku that protrudes from their heads and their colorful skin, which varies in each individual.

CULTURE

Twi'lek lekku can be used to communicate through subtle gestures in a form of sign language. This language is unique to the species and unlikely to be understood by outsiders. Lekku are very sensitive and can be very painful if damaged, but some Twi'leks tattoo their lekku with clan symbols.

Twi'leks believe very strongly in family and the legacy of their line. Each family has a Kalikori, which is a totem handed down from parent to child through the generations. Each parent adds to the artwork with unique elements, sometimes depicting key events, in order to leave their mark on their family's history.

Lekku: it's fascinating to watch Twi'leks communicate through these head-tails.

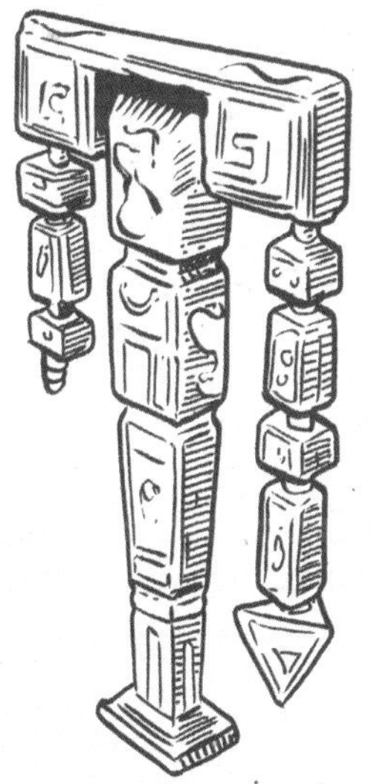

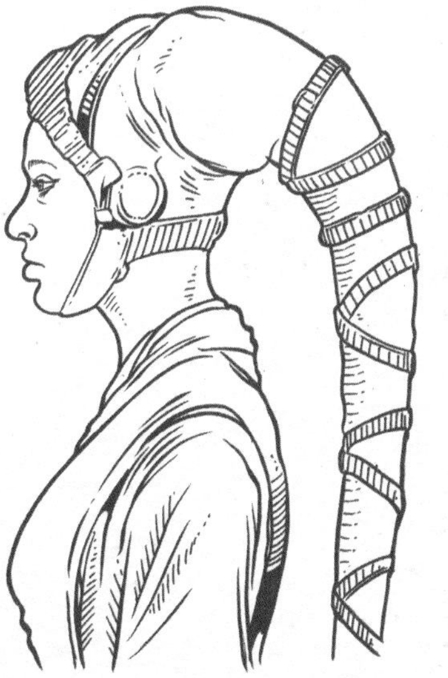

A Twi'lek let me see her family Kalikori, which depicted great battles of her ancestors.

TWI'LEKS IN THE GALAXY

Bib Fortuna was a male Twi'lek who served as majordomo in Jabba's palace for many years. As the head servant to the crime lord, Fortuna carried communications to Jabba's employees and guests, and helped keep his enemies in line with his stash of deadly poisons.

Cham Syndulla dedicated his whole life to fighting the rise of the Galactic Empire. He led the Twi'lek Resistance against the Separatists, and after his home planet fell under Imperial control, he dedicated himself to bringing about Ryloth's liberation. This courageous fighter was a skilled commander, and he was considered one of the greatest leaders of the Clone Wars.

Cham Syndulla's legacy was continued in his daughter Hera's own work for the Rebellion. Hera was the leader of a rebel cell called the Spectres. She was an excellent pilot and flew her starship, the *Ghost*, into many dangerous missions alongside her crew. Along with former Jedi Kanan Jarrus, she launched an insurgency against the Imperial occupation on the planet Lothal. Hera and her crew later joined another rebel cell under the guidance of Senator Bail Organa, who was at this time trying to coordinate the resistance effort all across the galaxy. The Spectres became one of the first groups to join the official Rebel Alliance as part of the larger Phoenix Squadron.

Aayla Secura was a brave Jedi Knight who was slain following Order 66. Secura was a revered leader in battle, serving as Jedi general of the Grand Army of the Republic. She had superior skills wielding her blue-bladed lightsaber.

KLATOOINIAN

HOMEWORLD: KLATOOINE

A sentient humanoid species, Klatooinians are a common sight throughout the galaxy. However, many of them are sold into slavery—presumably because their strong build makes them useful laborers. It is this same build and somewhat menacing appearance (caused in part by their prominent brow and visible teeth) that helps other Klatooinians find work as bounty hunters, henchmen, and bodyguards. Crime lord Jabba the Hutt employed a number of Klatooinian bodyguards, and a Klatooinian named Barada famously maintained the crime lord's skiffs. However, not all Klatooinians are drawn to the underworld. Some have been known to be Force-sensitive, and there were some Klatooinian Jedi Knights, such as Tarados Gon, that fought in the Battle of Geonosis.

I have met many Nikto in my travels—though I still can't get the names of the subspecies the right way around!

NIKTO

HOMEWORLD: KINTAN

Niktos are a common sight throughout the galaxy. They are a fascinating reptilian humanoid species, with subspecies that share many common traits, including scaly skin, facial horns, and glassy (almost blank) black eyes. Their main difference lies in their skin color. The two main subspecies are Kadas'sa'Niktos (green skin) and Kajain'sa'Niktos (red skin). They are particularly acclimatized to the desert and can often be seen on Tatooine—especially at the court of the notorious crime lord Jabba the Hutt. However, they can be found throughout the galaxy in a variety of roles—including that of Jedi. The notable Jedi Master Ima-Gun Di was a Nikto.

UMBARAN

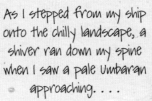

As I stepped from my ship onto the chilly landscape, a shiver ran down my spine when I saw a pale Umbaran approaching. . . .

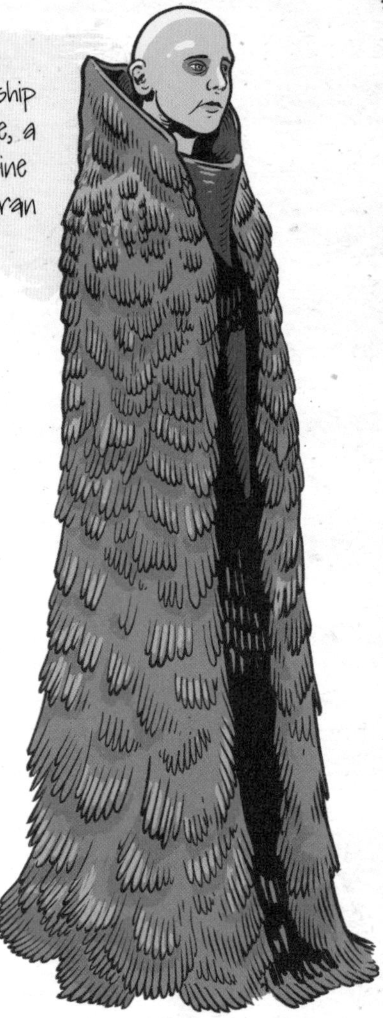

HOMEWORLD: UMBARA

Umbara is known as the Shadow World for good reason: light from the sun never completely reaches the planet's surface, leaving it constantly bathed in gloomy darkness. Umbarans have adapted to live in these conditions and are as cold and difficult to read as the planet itself. Humanoid in appearance, they have pale skin and colorless eyes that allow them to see ultraviolet light. Although perhaps not the most trustworthy, they are one of the most technologically advanced species in the galaxy. It is widely believed that they have the ability to subtly control others, perhaps making them perfect for politics. Sly Moore, a female Umbaran, served as Chancellor Palpatine's senior administrative aide for many years.

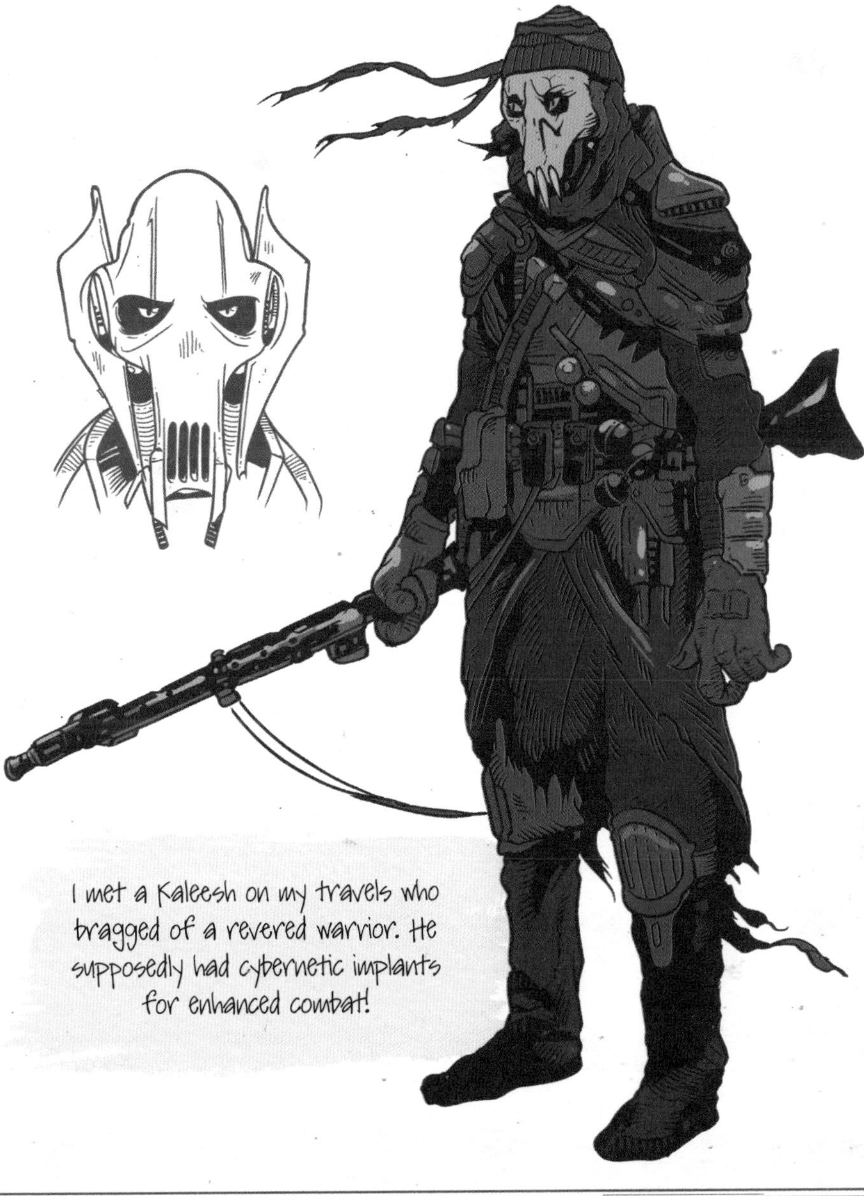

I met a Kaleesh on my travels who bragged of a revered warrior. He supposedly had cybernetic implants for enhanced combat!

KALEESH

HOMEWORLD: KALEE

Although perhaps not obvious at first glance, one of the most well-known (certainly most notorious) Kaleesh was General Grievous, the feared warrior who was so instrumental for the Separatists during the Clone Wars. Although an accident left him almost fully cybernetic, he still bore the trademark snakelike yellow eyes with slit pupils, flat nose, and elongated ears of his species. Generally, the Kaleesh have red skin, although they usually hide their faces beneath masks, and have an interesting way of walking on their toes as opposed to their entire feet. The pirate Sidon Ithano wears a Kaleesh helmet.

TOYDARIAN

HOMEWORLD: TOYDARIA

These winged, long-snouted creatures are known around the galaxy for their shrewd business sense, often making their living as merchants in bustling industrial hubs. The Toydarians have a reputation for being bad-tempered and miserly, but many possess a strong sense of pride in their work. They are one of the few species who can resist mental manipulation by users of the Force.

CULTURE

Toydaria is covered in swamps and forests, and its Royal City is perched on a mountain peak. The Toydarians live together in clans and make their homes in mud nests. Their wings enable them to fly almost anywhere, and the lack of vehicles on Toydaria allows them to take to the skies in relative safety. As a species they like to remain impartial in political matters, governed by a monarchy that liked to stay neutral during galactic disputes. During the Clone Wars, King Katuunko eventually agreed to side with the Republic after seeing the suffering caused by the conflict, but he was killed soon after for his choice.

Toydarian clan bell

Watto is a cheat. His chance cubes are loaded!

TOYDARIANS IN THE GALAXY

Watto, a Toydarian junk dealer, started his life as a soldier, but an injury forced him to seek out a new career. Arriving on Tatooine, he observed Jawas selling their used goods and decided to open his own shop in Mos Espa. He won two slaves from a Hutt in a bet, one of whom was Anakin Skywalker. Watto, a keen gambler, used Anakin's natural podracing abilities to his financial advantage but eventually lost his prize slave to Jedi Knight Qui-Gon Jinn in a wager on the Boonta Eve Classic.

⨁⨅⦚⦚⨍⨅⨂⦚⨅ KALLERAN

HOMEWORLD: KALLER

Kallerans are tall humanoids with aquatic features. Kaller was occupied by the Confederacy of Independent Systems, and the Kallerans were forced to provide workers and supplies. The Galactic Republic forces eventually defeated the Separatists and took control of Kaller, but many of the species could not see much of a difference.

Kallerans live on a world constantly occupied by enemy forces. Each one I have met has been resigned to their fate. I am not sure they know which side they are on in any given war.

⨅⦚⨅⦚⨂1 LANAI

HOMEWORLD: AHCH-TO

The females of the Lanai species are known as the Caretakers and are devoted to maintaining the sacred structures that dot the island home of the first Jedi temple. The males, known as Visitors, spend most of their time at sea, returning on a monthly basis with their catch. Their return is met with a celebration of dancing and music, which lasts for several days. Lanais lived harmoniously with Jedi Master Luke Skywalker, who sought refuge on Ahch-To after his quest to restore the Jedi Order failed. When Rey arrived to find Skywalker, she irritated the Lanais by being careless with the ancient landscape. While practicing her Force skills, she blew a hole in her hut and dropped a pillar on a Caretaker's wheelbarrow.

I heard stories of an aquatic planet tended to by an intelligent, peaceful species of gray creatures. It is rumored that these creatures—the Lanai—have lived on the sacred island for thousands of years.

ᛓᚲᚻᚻᛤᛉᛉᚲᚾ
BARDOTTAN

HOMEWORLD: BARDOTTA

Bardottans are scaled reptiles with long necks and beak-like snouts. Tall and short Bardottans make up two distinct races. They had a history of war until a group of Force-sensitive Bardottans, the Dagoyan Order, came to power and practiced a regime of religion and meditation. The Bardottans are now a species that values education and peace. Though a secretive society, some Bardottans do travel offworld in search of greater knowledge. Mars Guo was a famed podracer on Tatooine who participated at the Boonta Eve Classic.

Luggabeasts, cybernetically enhanced to weather the desert landscape.

ᛉᚢᚢᚲᚻᛤ
TEEDO

HOMEWORLD: JAKKU

Teedos spend their days as scavengers, traveling across the desert plains of their homeworld on the backs of luggabeasts, looking for sellable scrap. They wear mummy-like wrappings and a mask to protect against the harsh environment, which also gives them a menacing look. They are known to be aggressive and unpredictable, and fellow scavengers give them a wide berth. Teedos worship the goddess R'iia and believe the violent desert storms that bring famine and drought are her breath when she is angry.

Ion spear, for fighting and stunning rival scavengers.

ᚃᛕᛁᚅᚅᚢᛁᚴᚅᛁᚴᚐ

THISSPIASIAN

HOMEWORLD: THISSPIAS

This amazing species is noted for their thick hair and immensely strong tails, which can reach up to two meters in length. These striking features are not simply aesthetic. Thisspiasians use their strong tails to carry heavy objects and move quickly over rocky surfaces while their hair deters biting cygnats on their homeworld. They also possess mottled, reptilian skin and two pairs of hands that end in pointed, clawlike fingernails. Most Thisspiasians keep their second pair of hands concealed beneath their clothes. Despite being passionate beings, they keep their emotions well concealed under the guise of proud warrior. Descended from royalty on his homeworld, Oppo Rancisis was one such warrior and a celebrated Jedi.

A friendly Aleena excitedly recommended I see his friend, who was a famous podracer. He was well loved back on Aleen!

ᚴᛃᚍᛁᚍᛁᚐᚴ

ALEENA

HOMEWORLD: ALEEN

This blue, scaly-skinned species' main pursuits are friendship and peace. Aleena are very positive and welcoming to all who inhabit their homeworld, being very careful not to disrupt the mysterious creatures who live below the rocky surface on which they build their homes. Aleen's most famous native was the podracer Ratts Tyerell, who used his small stature and low weight to his advantage in the Boonta Eve Classic.

STEELPECKER

HOMEWORLD: JAKKU

These birds live in the desert wastelands of Jakku. They have iron-tipped beaks and talons, perfect for devouring their main food source. They are drawn to metal, feeding on materials like vanadium, osmiridium, and corundum. Though aggressive and prone to attack, steelpeckers are a desired commodity to scavengers, who collect their carcasses to retrieve the useful metals they consume.

NIGHTWATCHER WORM

HOMEWORLD: JAKKU

The mysterious nightwatcher worms are rarely seen but widely feared. They are also known as Arconan night terrors, because of their resemblance to the Arcona and their nightmarish activities. Living beneath the sands, they only emerge at night to hunt. Scavenger lore has it that they hunt by sensing vibrations above them, then rise up through the ground to engulf their prey. Only their terrifying red eyes give away their location.

The average nightwatcher worm is a terrifying twenty meters long!

WORRT

HOMEWORLD: TATOOINE

Worrts are nonsentient creatures that live in the desert and feed on rodents and insects. These squat creatures can bury themselves in the sand, becoming indistinguishable from the rocks around them, and there they will await their prey. Their oversized tongues are perfect for capturing food on the run.

Hiking farther across the rough terrain, I stubbed my toe on what I thought was a rock, until I heard a grunt. Looking down, I found a very angry creature embedded in the sandsand. . . .

WOMP RAT

HOMEWORLD: TATOOINE

These hideous rats are a common pest on Tatooine, where they have evolved to withstand the harsh desert climate. A breed of sharp-fanged rodent that can grow to just over two meters in length, they nest in the desert. They are not timid creatures and have been known to gather in swarms to attack luckless Tatooine inhabitants. Tusken Raiders use womp rat tusks to decorate their traditional clothing and accessories, while dewbacks enjoy them as a tasty treat. They can often be found in narrow ravines like Beggar's Canyon, where young skyhopper pilots use them for target practice.

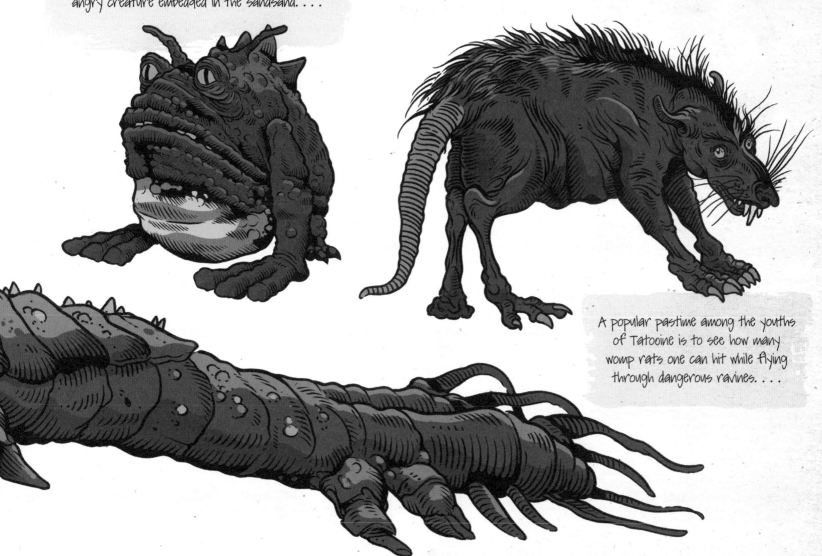

A popular pastime among the youths of Tatooine is to see how many womp rats one can hit while flying through dangerous ravines. . . .

NERF

HOMEWORLD: ALDERAAN

There seem to be quite a few disheveled nerf herders here on Alderaan. . . .

Nerfs are foul-smelling herd animals that are prized for their many uses. These four-legged, nonsentient animals, with their bodies covered in coarse, brown curly hair, curving horns, and lolling pink tongues, are a common sight throughout certain areas of the galaxy. They are raised for their milk, meat, and hide.

HAPPABORE

HOMEWORLD: JAKKU

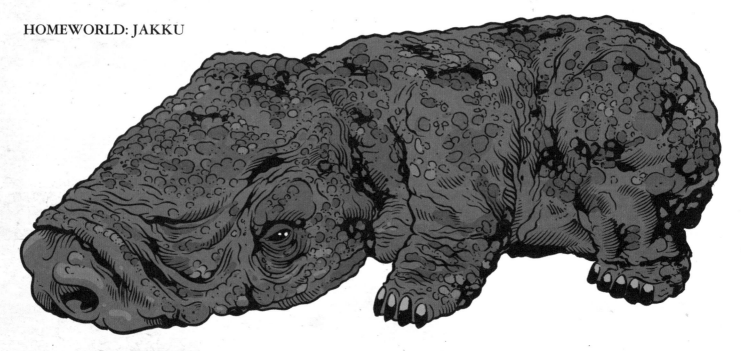

Happabores are large, gray herbivores with flat noses and beady eyes. They are known for being docile and obedient but are capable of violent defense if provoked. They can be found on many planets, pulling cargo or acting as mounts. They are slow but hardy, and can withstand inhospitable environments for long periods of time, making them ideal pack animals.

JERBA

HOMEWORLD: TATOOINE

With their horns and shaggy hair, jerbas are not the most attractive of creatures, but their strong and sturdy build makes them good beasts of burden in Tatooine's harsh desert conditions. They are also prized for their meat and milk, and their hides are widely used to make leather jewelry, boots, and rugs. They are a very useful creature indeed, which has apparently led to a smuggling trade in the animals.

An unpleasant smell floated to my nostrils as a herd of hairy, horned beasts shuffled past me.

BANTHA

HOMEWORLD: TATOOINE

Banthas are large, hairy mammals native to the deserts of Tatooine. They are bred all across the galaxy to be used as mounts, for their famous blue milk, which is used in butter, ice cream, and cheese, and for their meat. Their hides are often used in clothes and furniture. Sand People tame banthas, and each member has a special bond with their own mount.

RONTO

HOMEWORLD: TATOOINE

These gentle creatures are favored by Tatooine's famous Jawa traders because of their strength and loyalty to their owners. Not only are they able to carry heavy cargo, but their tall stature also serves to scare off Tusken Raiders. However, although they have excellent hearing and sense of smell, their eyesight is very poor, which means they can be startled by sudden movements. This has earned them the reputation of being slightly nervous creatures.

While in the bustling marketplace I learned, to my displeasure, that you should never try to ride a bucking ronto!

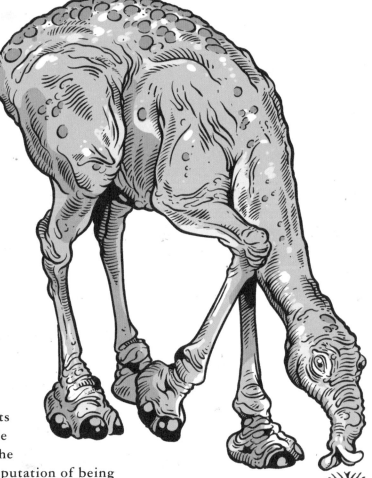

EOPIE

HOMEWORLD: TATOOINE

These four-legged herbivores are highly valued as beasts of burden on Tatooine. With their pale skin and flexible snouts, these tough, strong creatures have adapted to the planet's harsh desert conditions and have earned the reputation of being very dependable. Moisture farmers in particular use them to transport heavy loads.

DEWBACK

HOMEWORLD: TATOOINE

Dewbacks are thick-skinned reptiles used to carry heavy loads. They can withstand the desert heat from Tatooine's two suns, making them ideal mounts for the people of Mos Eisley. Merchants and moisture farmers use dewbacks to carry large loads, and sandtroopers use them whenever they need to patrol Tatooine.

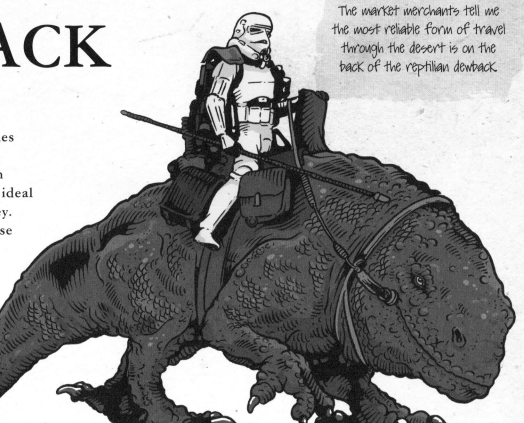

The market merchants tell me the most reliable form of travel through the desert is on the back of the reptilian dewback

LUGGABEAST

HOMEWORLD: JAKKU

Luggabeasts are mostly cybernetic and covered in heavy armor. Their masks are permanently fused to their faces, and mechanical systems enhance their ability to travel long journeys and carry heavy loads. They receive their nutrients directly via wires, so they do not require food or water. Teedos fit their luggabeasts with optical devices so they can locate droids and other valuable salvage.

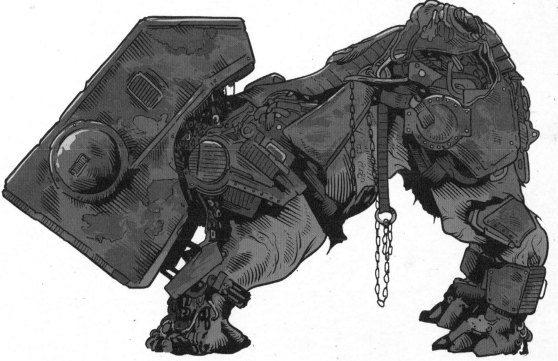

GUNDARK

HOMEWORLD: VANQOR

Famed throughout the galaxy for their fierceness and aggression, gundarks are mighty spectacles to behold. These red-skinned predators have sixteen razor-sharp claws, capable of easily tearing any prey apart. Their large nests are deadly to any invaders.

While I have always tried to see as many things as possible during my travels, I am pleased to say that I have never encountered a fearsome gundark! Not many who do so live to tell the tale.

LOTH-WOLF

HOMEWORLD: LOTHAL

These large canine predators were originally feared by the early settlers on the planet. However, they eventually came to be revered, and many now believe that the animals have a strong connection to the Force. Heavyset but able to move at great speed, with piercing eyes, they are truly magnificent but intimidating creatures. Early rebels on Lothal had a strong connection with the animals, particularly a giant white Loth-wolf.

The mysterious Loth-wolf is rumored to be so intelligent that it can speak Basic. I spent a long time on Lothal hoping to witness this phenomenon!

VARACTYL

HOMEWORLD: UTAPAU

Using long, powerful strides to traverse the rocky, sinkhole-pocked terrain of Utapau, these majestic reptavians are held in high esteem. With their beautiful blue-and-green plumage, head crest, and powerful tail, they are certainly a sight to behold. Their five-toed feet provide them with an excellent grip, which allows them to move swiftly across the ground or even vertically climb an obstacle, while the spines and feathered ridge along their backs provide defense. They also have very flexible necks and an armor-plated skull. The legendary Obi-Wan Kenobi chose a varactyl named Boga as his steed during his famous pursuit of General Grievous.

ANOOBA

HOMEWORLD: TATOOINE

While there are some documented cases of these animals being tamed (apparently the bounty hunter Embo owned a faithful one named Marrok), anoobas are generally extremely dangerous. In the wild, these carnivorous, fur-covered predators hunt in packs of between ten and twelve creatures. They have a prominent lower jaw, sharp fangs, chin tusks, and long claws, and they communicate via terrifying growls. When they catch their prey, they stab it with their chin tusks and then tear it apart. Renowned Jedi Master Even Piell was mortally wounded by a wild anooba as he tried to escape from the Citadel on Lola Sayu.

SARLACC

HOMEWORLD: TATOOINE

Sarlaccs are terrifying carnivorous beasts with giant tentacle-like appendages, massive mouths, and spear-like teeth. They live buried in the sand, feeding on any unlucky creatures that fall into their mouths. With an average length of one hundred meters and several stomachs, sarlaccs can swallow even the largest prey whole.

FEEDING

Once sarlaccs reach maturity after thirty thousand years, they burrow themselves one hundred meters below the sand. Their mouths remain closest to the surface, ready to devour their prey, while their most vital organs are protected beneath from other predators, such as the krayt dragon. The sarlaccs' tentacles are lightning-fast, allowing them to reach out and capture smaller prey, and they can also release an odor that attracts nearby herbivores to the pit.

SARLACCS IN THE GALAXY

Due to its proximity to Jabba the Hutt's palace, the Sarlacc in the Dune Sea is one of the crime lord's favorite pets. Unlike younger sarlaccs, who can move about to capture their food, this sarlacc stays in the same pit and awaits its prey. Jabba, using this convenient situation to his advantage, provides plenty of food in the form of his enemies. It is in the ideal spot for an execution, and Jabba and his guests happily travel to the pit to watch the event.

⊐⊐⋉⋁↓ ⊐⊐⋉⊐⌂⋀

KRAYT DRAGON

HOMEWORLD: TATOOINE

Known for their ferocity and with an average length of five meters, krayt dragons are the apex predators of the desert. However, despite their frightening size, krayt dragons are hunted ruthlessly for the highly valuable pearls they produce. Sand People and Jawas who conquer such beasts are held in high regard by their people.

⋌⋉⋁⋁⋀⊬±

MASSIFF

HOMEWORLD: TATOOINE AND GEONOSIS

These four-legged, canine-like creatures native to desert worlds are often domesticated for various purposes. Desert-dwelling species, such as the Tusken Raiders, are fond of using them for sentry and guard tasks. Their large yellow eyes give them good night vision, making it easier for them to spot approaching enemies, while the spines along their humped backs provide an extra level of defense. Clone troopers have also been known to employ the creatures as trackers.

ᑫᑫᑌ· ᑌᑫᐢ

PAU'AN

HOMEWORLD: UTAPAU

I met a Pau'an once in a cantina on Coruscant. Like so many of his kind, he had fled his homeworld after it was occupied by the Empire and sought refuge in the bustling capital.

Pau'ans are tall humanoids with gaunt faces, sharp teeth, and heightened senses. They have an extremely long lifespan measured in centuries, which gained them the nickname the Ancients. Despite their frightening appearance, Pau'ans are a mostly peaceful species, and they can communicate in Basic as well as their native Utapese.

CULTURE

The Pau'ans tame the local varactyls, a quick, feathered species, to ride and transport cargo through their underground cities. Utapau is shared with the Amani and the Utai, a shorter species of humanoids who live in caverns under the planet's surface. The Pau'ans and the Utai merged in society when the climate aboveground forced the Pau'ans to abandon their surface dwellings. Pau'ans have hypersensitive vision, so they are happy to live in darkness, building their cities in the sinkholes on the remote planet of Utapau.

PAU'ANS IN THE GALAXY

The most notable Pau'an in galactic history held the position of Jedi Temple guard (before the Clone Wars). This position had an ancient heritage and required the highest level of dedication and service. This Pau'an abandoned his duty to defend the Order and turned to the dark side of the Force. He became the head of the Inquisitors, a group of Force-sensitive beings whose mission was to hunt down any Jedi who survived the purge of Order 66. As Grand Inquisitor, this anonymous Pau'an took a particular interest in destroying the rebel cell known as the Spectres. He wanted to defeat the escaped Jedi Kanan Jarrus and his young Padawan, Ezra Bridger. Having studied the Jedi Archives to understand Jedi fighting styles, the Grand Inquisitor was an almost unbeatable opponent, especially with his double-bladed spinning lightsaber.

The Utapaun trident is a melee weapon used by Pau'an warriors.

This forked spear includes a blaster that fires green bolts through its prongs.

ꜱꞀꞀꞀꞀꜱꞀꞀ

SULLUSTAN

HOMEWORLD: SULLUST

A curious-looking smuggler helped me fix my ship at a spaceport in the Outer Rim. This friendly sullustan was a skilled pilot himself and gave me some tips for my onward journey.

Sullustans are a species of short humanoids recognizable by the jowls around their cheeks. As a species, they have a natural talent for mechanical and technological tasks. Friendly and pragmatic, they are well-known throughout the galaxy and have contributed to many galactic events with their inventions and advancements in engineering.

CULTURE

Sullust is a highly toxic, volcanic world, so Sullustans build their cities underground, using lifts and shuttles to carry them to and from work. More than half the population works for the SoroSuub Corporation, an advanced technology manufacturer that develops droids, sensors, weapons, vehicles, and much more. Sullustans are considered experts in technological development and economics, and SoroSuub sells its wares all over the galaxy.

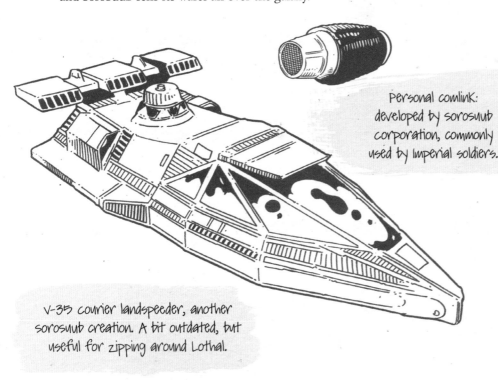

Personal comlink: developed by sorosuub corporation, commonly used by Imperial soldiers.

V-35 courier landspeeder, another sorosuub creation. A bit outdated, but useful for zipping around Lothal.

SULLUSTANS IN THE GALAXY

Due to their affinity for technology, Sullustans are ideal candidates for positions within military organizations. When the Empire began mining Sullust for fuel, the Rebel Alliance began to recruit Sullustans for their fleet. Nien Nunb, a former smuggler, agreed to aid his friends within the Alliance by smuggling Alderaanians, including Princess Leia Organa, off Sullust to avoid detection by the Empire. He later flew as Lando Calrissian's copilot on the *Millennium Falcon* during the Battle of Endor.

LASAT

HOMEWORLD: LIRA SAN

Lasats are a large, humanoid species known for their impressive strength and agility. Their hands and feet are ideal for climbing, and they have superior sight and hearing. Due to their height, strength, and aggression in combat, Lasats are sometimes mistaken for hairless Wookiees—a comparison that does not please either species!

CULTURE

Lasats originated on the remote planet of Lira San. This hidden world in Wild Space was all but forgotten, with many believing the Lasats' native home was Lasan. The inhabitants of Lasan had forgotten about their ancestral home, despite millions of their species still living there. Lasan itself was devastated when Imperial forces invaded and killed most of its population. The survivors of the Siege of Lasan were forced to flee and colonize other worlds.

Though not Force-sensitive, Lasats believe in the light side of the Force and practice a peaceful lifestyle. Despite their reliance on physical prowess, they hold knowledge in high regard. Fighting skills are also revered among the Lasat people. The most capable among them are trained to join the Lasan Honor Guard, a military organization developed to protect the Lasan royal family. The soldiers need to be highly intelligent, be agile, and have excellent combat skills.

WEAPONS

The Lasan Honor Guard carry unique weapons called AB-75 bo-rifles. They feature a blaster barrel, bayonet, and electromagnetic pulse-generator tip. Guards have to be highly trained to wield the bo-rifle as it requires a great deal of skill and strength. If a guard is bested in combat, it is the Lasat way to surrender their weapon to the victor.

LASATS IN THE GALAXY

Following the fall of Lasan, very few Lasats were left in the galaxy. The most notable survivor was Garazeb Orrelios. Zeb, as he was more commonly known, was captain of the Lasan Honor Guard. When the Imperials came to decimate Lasan, Zeb was charged with protecting the royal family. They did not survive, but Zeb escaped Lasan with a deep hatred of the Empire. He joined a rebel cell called the Spectres and traveled with them aboard the *Ghost* on missions to disrupt the Empire's plans on the planet Lothal. Zeb was an excellent addition to their crew as he could act as the muscle and do a lot of the heavy lifting.

When the *Ghost* crew arrived to rescue them from Imperial arrest, two Lasat refugees told Zeb they were going to Lira San, their ancestral home. Zeb, like many Lasat exiles, believed Lira San was only a legend. The refugees told him of a prophecy, which they interpreted to mean that Zeb could find Lira San using his bo-rifle. Zeb agreed to perform the ritual, and following a difficult journey, the group found their original homeworld populated with millions of Lasat. Zeb vowed to guide other surviving Lasats to Lira San and reunite the species.

Their bo-rifle closely resembles the old clone troopers' electrostaff with its electrified tip.

I was able to see an AB-75 bo-rifle, the sacred weapon of the Lasats, despite the fact they have rarely been seen following the destruction of Lasan.

TATOOINE

I found myself on a sparsely populated desert planet, with twin suns beating down on my neck. I was desperate for refreshment and unnerved by the vast sheet of sand in front of me. My ship had crashed and was in need of parts, and my companion droid had shut down from overheating.

Thankfully, I spied a merchant atop a green reptilian mount and followed him to a lively cantina, full of music and mischief. Here, a wookiee growled triumphantly in the background, a band of jazzy Bith played a jaunty tune, and an Aqualish tried to start a fight.

I left the cantina to attend a podrace. The arena was filled with competitors and spectators from all over the galaxy. A couple of Jawas tried to sell me a faulty droid on the way in, and I placed my bet with a very argumentative Toydarian.

I later wandered to a place far up in the Dune sea, where I gained entrance to a crime lord's palace. After a game of cards with a fierce bounty hunter, I snuck into the surrounding passages for a quick look around. What I found scared me to death, and I ran screaming from the palace, never to return again.

MOS EISLEY

The cantina in Mos Eisley was a puzzling sight for those unused to travel. This dimly lit watering hole played host to aliens of all shapes and sizes—some large and particularly frightening! If you avoided the occasional violent outbreaks, it was a great place to grab a drink and listen to some music. The bar was lined with bounty hunters looking for their next job, and spies hid in the dark corners.

CHADRA-FAN

HOMEWORLD: CHAD

Chadra-Fan are short, furry humanoids with large ears and flat noses. They are quick-witted with acute senses, which make them highly perceptive beings. Kabe, a female Chadra-Fan, was a regular at the Mos Eisley cantina. She used an annoying high-pitched squeak to attract the attention of the bartender. Shortpaw, a male Chadra-Fan who operated during the Galactic Civil War, was the leader of a secret organization consisting of smugglers and mercenaries.

MORSEERIAN

HOMEWORLD: MERJ

Morseerians have four arms and a methane-based respiratory system, meaning they have to wear curious environment suits and masks when traveling to oxygen-based planets. Not much is known about this secretive species' homeworld, history, or culture, but some members did gain fame in the wider galaxy. Nabrun Leids was a successful smuggler and pilot for hire, whose ship was a custom-made freighter called the *Scarlet Vertha*.

WHIPHID

HOMEWORLD: TOOLA

Whiphids are covered in a thick layer of fur to protect them from the icy climate of their home planet. They have an intimidating appearance with heights of up to two and a half meters, large sharp tusks, and primitive dress. They are excellent hunters, but lack the technology of more advanced species. This inspires many to leave Toola to use their skills elsewhere in the galaxy as game or bounty hunters. Valarian, a female Whiphid, became Jabba the Hutt's main rival on Tatooine. Her partner, J'Quille, was sent to spy in Jabba's palace with the goal of poisoning the crime lord's food. While he was there, he witnessed the arrival and capture of Leia Organa, who had come to rescue Han Solo.

You do not want to get on the wrong side of a whiphid. Those tusks look deadly!

ᒍᐑᒪᑕᗡᒿᗝᒷᒿ

LAMPROID

HOMEWORLD: FLORN

Lamproids are carnivorous predators with thick necks and large teeth. They are well adapted to the dangerous environment of their homeworld, protecting themselves against other predators with their teeth, serpentine coils, and venomous tails. They are aggressive, and with no obvious culture or creative pursuits, are often mistaken as nonsentient. Dice Ibegon was a Force-sensitive Lamproid and member of the Rebel Alliance.

some of the bar patrons looked very aggressive. I was afraid to approach one serpentine character, but he turned out to be a friendly rebel ally.

ᒍᐑᒿᗢᗡ

TALZ

HOMEWORLD: ORTO PLUTONIA

Talz hail from icy plains where strong winds and constant snow prevail. Their shaggy fur coats protect them from the harsh climate, and they survive living a simple existence, using few tools and no technology. Until the time of the Galactic Civil War, the Talz did not have the advancements for space travel or complex weaponry, but defended their native land with primitive spears and animal instincts. Muftak was a male Talz who operated as a pickpocket on Mos Eisley and frequented the cantina.

I think this furry guy was pretty far from home. His thick coat was not designed for the hot twin suns.

AQUALISH

HOMEWORLD: ANDO

Aqualish are sentient humanoids, identifiable by the large tusks that stick out of their jaws. Not all Aqualish look alike though, as the number of eyes and fingers varies. They are not known for being peaceful and often seek careers as mercenaries, bounty hunters, and pirates. Many Aqualish aligned themselves with the Confederacy of Independent Systems during the Galactic Republic. Quarrelsome and thug-like, the Aqualish culture revolves around aggression and toughness, with diplomacy being one of their weakest attributes. Ponda Baba was in a criminal partnership with the nefarious cryptosurgeon Evazan. The two were employed as smugglers by the crime lord Jabba the Hutt. While on Tatooine, Ponda Baba patronized the local cantina and drunkenly picked a fight with a young Luke Skywalker. Obi-Wan Kenobi swiftly removed Baba's arm with his lightsaber, putting an end to the argument.

I tried to talk to some of the patrons at the bar, but the aggression from one particular alien with unusual pink tusks protruding from his face forced me away from the area. The Aqualish people are not fond of questions. . : .

ITHORIAN

HOMEWORLD: ITHOR

Commonly referred to as hammerheads, Ithorians are believed to be a peaceful and unique-looking species. They spend their time philosophizing and tending their forest gardens, detesting violence and revering nature. Ithorians have two mouths and four throats, so they speak in stereo. Momaw Nadon was exiled from his home planet after revealing agricultural secrets to the Empire, though he believed he was doing it to save Ithor. He spent his exile on Tatooine, despite the arid planet being quite different from the lush Ithor.

⊟1↓⊟

BITH

HOMEWORLD: BITH (ALSO KNOWN AS CLAK'DOR VII)

The Bith are an intelligent species with hairless, dome-shaped heads and extremely sensitive hearing. They can be found galaxywide at all levels of society, fully adapted to a civilized, high-technology lifestyle. The Bith remained loyal to the Republic throughout the Clone Wars, but as a peaceful species, they stayed away from the fight.

CULTURE

The Bith can be traced back millions of years, possibly making them one of the galaxy's most ancient civilizations. They have a long-standing history of sending their Force-sensitive members to join the Jedi Order. The Bith can be found on many planets, engaged in many different pursuits. Their natural intelligence leads to careers in engineering, politics, science, and academics. Their exceptional hearing also lends itself to a natural ability in music.

BITH IN THE GALAXY

Some of the most famous of the Bith's musical members are Figrin D'an and his band, the Modal Nodes. They play in the cantina in Mos Eisley to a rowdy crowd of smugglers and spacers. The seven-member group is key in keeping up the spirits of weary travelers and ensuring the mood is light in the cantina whatever the political atmosphere outside.

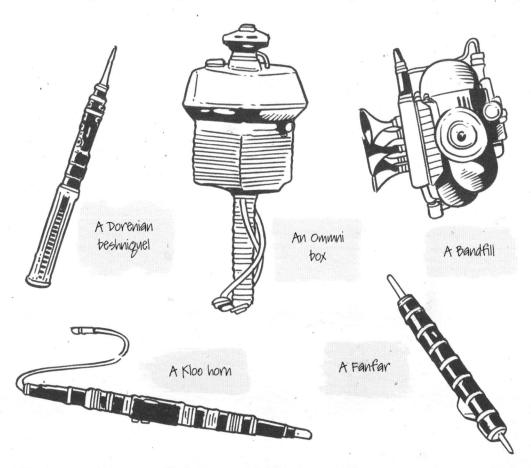

A Dorenian beshniquel

An Ommni box

A Bandfill

A Kloo horn

A Fanfar

RODIAN

HOMEWORLD: RODIA

Rodians, a reptilian species from the Tyrius system, are well-known around the galaxy. Many infamous bounty hunters hail from their culture, which is notoriously violent and drawn to criminal activity. Despite this nature, the Rodians produced many artists, scientists, and politicians, as well as some loyal to noble causes in the Republic and Rebel Alliance.

HABITAT

Rodia is a remote jungle planet covered in thick bogs. Though Rodians evolved to build their cities on waterways protected by environmental shields, they still display features of swamp-dwelling species, such as suction pads on their fingers allowing them to climb aquatic vegetation. As the Rodians develop more technological capabilities, their natural rainforest environment becomes more endangered, with smaller fauna and flora dying out completely.

RODIANS IN THE GALAXY

One of the most famous Rodian stories features a bounty hunter named Greedo. He worked for Jabba the Hutt on Tatooine, capturing his adversaries, chasing down debts, and carrying out various other criminal endeavors. Impulsive and quick to anger, Greedo was not always the right person for the job, and he met his end when he picked a fight with a rogue smuggler named Han Solo.

Rodians are not all thugs for hire. In the last years of the Galactic Republic, Senator Onaconda Farr represented his home planet, fighting the famine that had plagued his people. Bolla Ropal was a Jedi Master and the keeper of a kyber memory crystal, which held the identity of all the Force-sensitive children in the galaxy. He died protecting it from the bounty hunter Cad Bane. Ganodi was training to be a Jedi. She and her fellow initiates rescued Ahsoka Tano when she was captured by Weequay pirates. A Rodian was also a member of the gang of marauders known as the Cloud-Riders. Led by Enfys Nest, these pirates plundered cargo ships in the Outer Rim.

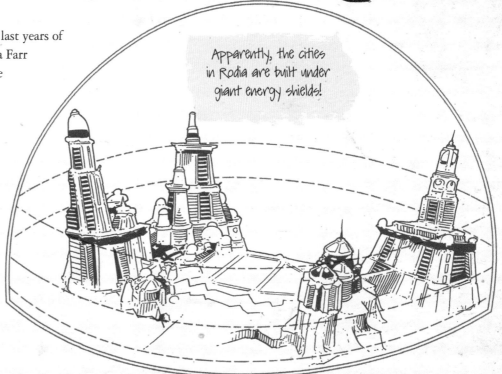

Apparently, the cities in Rodia are built under giant energy shields!

⌂⌂⌂⌐1⋁⋀⋁

WOOKIEE

HOMEWORLD: KASHYYYK

Wookiees are a forest-dwelling species with thick fur and long, sharp claws. They stand at over two and a half meters tall and have immense strength and a long lifespan. Though few people speak their native language, and they themselves do not speak Galactic Basic, they are widely regarded as an intelligent and loyal species.

WEAPONS AND ARMORY

The traditional weapon of the Wookiee species is the bowcaster. Each warrior handcrafts a unique weapon, but they all feature two magnetic polarizers that charge the quarrel, sending a blast bolt from the barrel. In large battles, Wookiees also carry a sidearm blaster. These are durable and reliable, and copper-colored like all traditional Wookiee technology. Decorative pauldrons with traditional clan designs and handcrafted helmets and shields make a Wookiee stand out on the battlefield, as well as protecting vital body parts.

Bowcaster: the unique and powerful weapon of the Wookiee warrior.

The Kashyyyk clarion horn is a musical instrument used in Wookiee gatherings.

CULTURE

From a young age, Wookiees are encouraged to develop the artistic skills for which the species is renowned. They craft objects from natural materials—some decorative and traditional for use in cultural ceremonies, and others combined with technology for practical use. As well as creative pursuits, the Wookiees enjoy games and competition. However, their sometimes-aggressive nature can make it safer for weaker species to always remember the mantra: Let the Wookiee win.

Wookiees are extremely honorable. They do, however, have terrifying tempers that, when ignited, can lead to frightening consequences for their adversaries. They never go to war for trivial reasons but are fierce warriors in protection of their allies. They suffered greatly at the hands of the Empire, which subjugated their homeworld and used Wookiees as slaves.

WOOKIEES IN THE GALAXY

One of the most famous Wookiees in the galaxy was the rebel hero Chewbacca. Chewie, as he was more affectionately known, served as Han Solo's copilot on board the *Millennium Falcon*. The two became best friends after escaping Imperial capture on Mimban and went on to make the Kessel Run in record time. During an early mission on Kessel, Chewie went against orders to rescue his fellow Wookiees, who had been enslaved by the Empire. Later, Chewie was a vital member of the Rebel Alliance, fighting alongside Luke Skywalker against the evil Empire. After the fall of the Empire, Chewie returned to a smuggler's life with Han, only to be called back to the fight when the Resistance needed help against the rising First Order. Chewie was known for his great bravery and often served as Han's conscience throughout their friendship. He remained loyal to Han until the human's sad demise.

ꟻ𝖵𝖸𝖪𝟽𝟶𝖴𝟷𝖪𝖴

DEVARONIAN

HOMEWORLD: DEVARON

Devaronians are a humanoid species. The males are bald with
horns, and the females have a full head of hair with small bumps
instead of horns. The Devaronian society is based around a
matriarchal government, where the males aren't allowed to hold
office. Females are serious-minded and stay on planet, and the
males long to wander the stars.

𝖴𝖴𝟷𝖸𝖸𝟷𝖪𝖴

SNIVVIAN

HOMEWORLD: CADOMAI PRIME

Snivvians are thick-skinned humanoids
with large mouths and short fangs.
The winters on their home planet
are long and hard to survive, and the
Snivvians spend the time in artistic
pursuits in underground caverns. Some
of the species escape the icy tundras to
become bounty hunters offworld. As
a species they display great tracking
skills, so they are particularly suited to
this work. Sinrich was a well-known
bounty hunter during the Clone Wars.
He invented the holographic disguise
matrix, which allowed users to disguise
themselves as someone else. Zutton, a
Snivvian artist, frequented the cantina
in Mos Eisley with his brother Takeel.
They, like most Snivvians, were often
nicknamed snaggletooths because of
their protruding jaws.

I met a couple of
snaggletooths in the cantina
looking for work. Their thick
hides were unsuited to the
heat in the desert!

54

DUROS

HOMEWORLD: DURO

Duros are humanoids with blue-green skin and red eyes. They are known for being storytellers, with many of this adventurous species traveling and exploring the galaxy. During the Clone Wars, the Duros Cad Bane accelerated to become the leading bounty hunter, with excellent combat skills, specifically against Jedi. He was known to be equipped with a pair of blaster pistols, rocket boots, and a wide-brimmed hat.

> Hard to miss a Duros. Those red eyes can haunt your dreams!

LL-30 blaster pistols

> I sat down for a game of cards with a vuvrian. I heard she was a spy, so I quickly moved on.

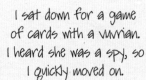

VUVRIAN

HOMEWORLD: VURDON KA

Vuvrians are humanoids with twelve-eyed, insect-like heads. They are well-known across the galaxy for their diplomacy as well as their excellent sales and negotiation skills. As a species, they never colonize other worlds, preferring to stay on their own peaceful homeworld. Vuvrians also have heightened senses, which make them particularly observant, and many Vuvrians excelled in the Jedi Order.

PODRACING

Podracing was a big deal on Tatooine. The events drew crowds from all over the galaxy. The competitors were often famous, and the prizes were sizable. I joined the other spectators just as a Xexto pilot whizzed around a sharp turn and slammed into a large rock face.

ᔑᏈᎧ᎗Ꮘ

TROIG

HOMEWORLD: POLLILLUS

I was unable to concentrate on the commentary. I couldn't stop staring at the two-headed announcer!

Troigs are instantly identifiable by their two heads and four arms. Each head of a Troig has its own personality and temperament. Both heads share the same awareness, and they are therefore very alert and observant. They are a clever and curious species, able to learn many languages, and have produced plenty of great scientists. The heads of a Troig have individual names, but they can be combined for clarity. For example, Fodesinbeed is an amalgamation of the great podracing announcer's two heads, Fode and Beed. Fode and Beed provided commentary on the sport in two different languages.

TOONG

HOMEWORLD: TUND

Toongs are an unusual-looking species, with giant heads, no torsos, and antennae sprouting from their heads. They are extremely timid, preferring the company of their own families and avoiding confrontation with the wider galaxy. One Toong was able to overcome his shyness and become a podracer on Tatooine. Ben Quadinaros participated in the Boonta Eve Classic alongside a young Anakin Skywalker. During the race, Quadinaros's podracer malfunctioned and his engines exploded.

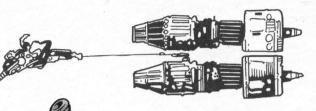

Ben Quadinaros's pod has four engines.

The Toong pilot was rumored to be one to watch, but his podracer soon malfunctioned and put him out of the competition.

NUKNOG

HOMEWORLD: SUMP

Nuknogs are reptilian humanoids with bulbous heads and small brains. They have short tempers, and their diminished brain capacity means they are not often very successful in society. Ark Roose, also known as Bumpy, was a particularly dim-witted Nuknog who competed as a podracer on Tatooine. His strategy on the course was to simply crash into his opponents, often resulting in his own hospitalization.

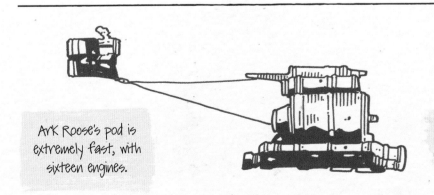

Ark Roose's pod is extremely fast, with sixteen engines.

Dim-witted species, no chance of winning.

⊐⊔⊔ DUG

HOMEWORLD: MALASTARE

Dugs are easily identified by their long snouts and their unique walk. They use their hands to get around while their legs hang in the air. Dugs live in tribes on Malastare, where they work together to exploit their homeworld's vast fuel reserves. One of the best-known Dugs was Sebulba, who left Malastare to become a famous podracer on Tatooine.

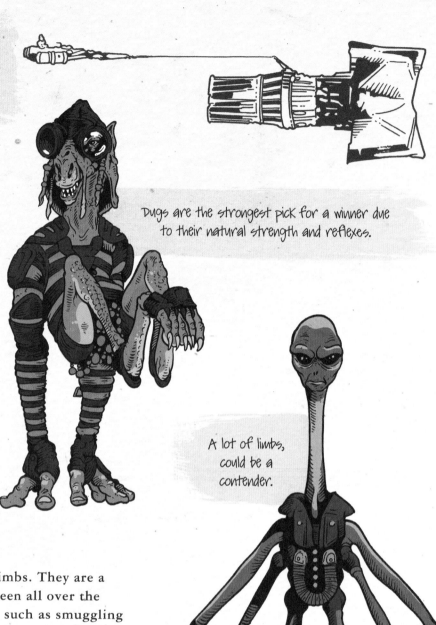

Sebulba's racer is packed with tricks to help him win.

Dugs are the strongest pick for a winner due to their natural strength and reflexes.

A lot of limbs, could be a contender.

△∨△↓△ XEXTO

HOMEWORLD: TROIKEN

Xexto are recognizable by their six spindly limbs. They are a highly dexterous species, and Xexto can be seen all over the galaxy using these extra limbs in professions such as smuggling and pickpocketing, but they are also able to participate in the dangerous sport of podracing. Due to their extra appendages, they are adept at using slingshots as weapons, and these are very popular in Xexto culture. During the last decades of the Republic, a Xexto named Gasgano competed in the Boonta Eve Classic. He piloted a green Ord Pedrovia podracer, using all his arms to control the vehicle, but despite running a competitive race, he ultimately lost to Force-sensitive Anakin Skywalker.

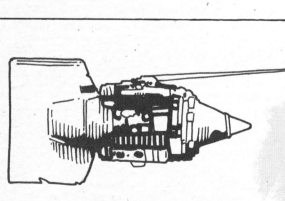

Rumor has it, Gasgano's pod has a built-in camera that allows him to see behind him.

ER'KIT

HOMEWORLD: ER'KIT

The Er'Kits are a blue-gray humanoid species with a murky history, thanks to their homeworld's ties to political scandal, the slave trade, and violent militia. They possess large, elongated skulls and very long, skinny legs, and they have adapted so well to desert-world conditions that many Er'Kit can be found on Tatooine. Two famed Er'Kits were the corrupt senator Danry Ledwellow and the more popular podracer Ody Mandrell, who memorably took part in the Boonta Eve Classic.

Ody Mandrell's racer has a simple but speedy engine.

I don't think the Er'Kit's long legs lend themselves very easily to the tight space of a podracer, but this one put up a good fight before his eventual defeat.

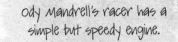

FLUGGRIAN

HOMEWORLD: PLOO IV

Fluggrians have a very distinctive appearance, with green-and-purple skin, spikes protruding from their arms and heads, and yellow eyes. Elan Mak was a podracer in the Boonta Eve Classic on Tatooine, where he finished the race in fifth place.

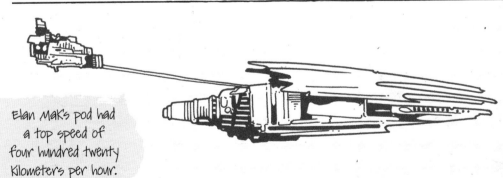

Elan Mak's pod had a top speed of four hundred twenty kilometers per hour.

The Fluggrian competitor stayed in the middle of the pack, cleverly avoiding collisions.

JABBA'S PALACE

As I headed up the old dirt road through the arid canyon, an old monastery came into view. The home of the most notorious gangster in Tatooine was a sandblasted metal structure with curved roofs and was rumored to have been fortified by master armorers. It is extremely hard to get inside, but I used my underworld connections to secure a place at a card game in the throne room.

KITONAK

HOMEWORLD: KIRDO III

The music in the palace was provided by some interesting creatures who didn't look like they really wanted to be there. . . .

The Kitonak have thick skin that offers protection from harsh climates. They also have tiny eyes that are hidden by folds of skin, and their bodies release a strange, vanilla-like smell. A Kitonak's true name is actually a series of whistles, which can only be pronounced by other Kitonak. Droopy McCool was a Kitonak musician who played his Chidinkalu flute in Max Rebo's band.

ᴑᴆᴊᴑᴊᴋᴧ
ORTOLAN

HOMEWORLD: ORTO

Ortolans are squat, blue-skinned bipeds who have large, floppy ears and a trunk-like nose. Lacking arms, they perform basic functions such as eating and drinking using their toes. Their native planet is very cold, so they consume large amounts of food to develop a warm layer of blubber. Max Rebo, a male Ortolan, used his two legs to play the red ball jet organ in his own band, often for criminals like Jabba the Hutt.

The Yuzzum in Jabba's band had the most beautiful singing voice, a talent for which the species is known.

ᴠᴑᴆᴆᴑᴌ
YUZZUM

HOMEWORLD: ENDOR

Yuzzums are odd-looking, furry creatures with very long legs for running quickly across the plains of Endor. They tame rakazzak beasts to use as mounts and ride them when hunting rodents hidden in the tall grass. They only have very simple tools and technology but have a rich culture of music, food, and wine. The wine they brew is so potent that non-Yuzzums must mix it with the sweeter wine of fellow Endor inhabitants the Ewoks. Yuzzums are excellent singers, and during the last years of the Galactic Empire, Joh Yowza left Endor and went to Tatooine, where he often performed with the Max Rebo band. He was a particular favorite of crime lord Jabba the Hutt.

ᗱᏌ↓↓

HUTT

HOMEWORLD: NAL HUTTA

I spotted the owner of the palace from a distance, surrounded by sycophants, and many I believed were being held against their will. Some of the patrons whispered to me of the great Hutt dynasty and that no one argues with Jabba if they don't want to be fed to his pets. I was pleased to leave this lavish palace in one piece.

Hutts, well-known throughout the galaxy for their notorious criminal enterprises, are a typically obese species with slimy skin and stubby arms. They can live for centuries and grow to terrifying sizes. Large families spanning generations serve the Hutt crime syndicate, which keeps a tight hold over many territories across the galaxy.

CULTURE

Criminal behavior is deeply entrenched in Huttese culture. The Hutts are notorious gangsters and swindlers, often trading in slaves, weapons, and other illegal ventures. The Grand Hutt Council, operating from Nal Hutta, is made up of high-ranking members of the species and oversees all criminal activity. Many Hutts live opulent lifestyles funded by their gangster businesses, living in lavish palaces with all the best food, drink, and entertainment they could want. They have large teams of staff for service, security, and amusement.

The Hutt Clan is divided into large families, and each member has tattoos to show their allegiance. There is much infighting and scheming among them, grasping for territories, wealth, and power. Loyalty to one's family is paramount in Hutt society. Most Hutts consider their native language of Huttese to be superior to all others and, even though they are more than capable of learning it, refuse to speak in Galactic Basic.

HUTTS IN THE GALAXY

Jabba Desilijic Tiure was a major figure on Tatooine, controlling the planet's illegal trade and piracy from his grand palace in the Northern Dune Sea. His influence across the Outer Rim territories gained him a seat on the Grand Hutt Council, and he spent most of the Galactic Republic years through the rise of the Empire as the reigning crime lord of the region.

His palace was an old monastery accessible only by a single dirt road through a canyon. It was fortified by master armorers and full of traps, beasts, and prisons for his many enemies. Jabba also kept a malfunctioning droid that enjoyed torturing fellow machines to run his cyborg operations.

The palace would always be filled with Jabba's network of smugglers, arms dealers, slavers, staff, and guests, whom he would entertain in his elaborate throne room. Jabba was renowned for his parties, with famous musicians and high-stakes gambling. The host's violent tendencies could also be enjoyed as a spectator sport when Jabba would toss his adversaries into the rancor pit.

Jabba would sometimes travel in style on the *Khetanna*, a sail barge manufactured by Ubrikkian Industries. This grand vehicle would carry Jabba and his guests to the Great Pit of Carkoon, where, when the rancor just wouldn't do, enemies would be thrown into the jaws of the terrifying Sarlacc.

The wealthiest Hutt families favored grand sail barges to travel about their territories.

KOWAKIAN MONKEY-LIZARD

HOMEWORLD: KOWAK

Kowakian monkey-lizards are small, intelligent creatures often kept as pets. They are considered entertaining by members of the underworld due to their cruel sense of humor. Most notably, one was employed as a court jester by the famed crime lord Jabba the Hutt. Salacious B. Crumb was tasked with amusing the gangster at least once every day in exchange for his life. He successfully survived in Jabba's court for many years, eating and drinking as much as he liked and entertaining his master by mimicking and teasing his guests and captives.

This sarcastic monkey-lizard performed skits at Jabba's feet. He mocked the guests and reveled in Jabba's hideous laughter.

ELOM

HOMEWORLD: ELOM

Despite their mysterious origins, Eloms are known to inhabit frozen grottos. They are short and covered in thick, oily fur, suitable for colder climates. As a result of living in darkness, Eloms have exceptional eyesight but find natural or bright lights intolerable. Though as a species they rarely venture outside their caves, one Elom did make a name for himself offworld. Tanus Spijek was a spy for the Rebel Alliance during the Galactic Civil War.

⟨Aurebesh⟩

RANCOR

HOMEWORLD: UNKNOWN

Enormous and terrifying, rancors are formidable predators. Standing at five meters tall and weighing over fifteen hundred kilograms, they can withstand most attacks, including blaster fire. Though these beasts are the most unlikely pets, Jabba the Hutt kept one in his palace. He used the rancor to punish his enemies, which was also a source of entertainment for his guests.

I noticed a door to a dark corridor and decided to explore some more of the palace. I found myself near a dungeon where a guard was trying to wrangle a large creature on a leash. When I looked up, I saw the biggest, scariest creature I've ever seen!

GAMORREAN

> There were porcine guards all over the palace. They looked menacing but simple enough to fool.

HOMEWORLD: GAMORR

The violent, war-loving Gamorreans have porcine traits, including hulking bodies, large snouts, and tusks. The females are referred to as sows and the males as boars. They are not very intelligent, and their native language is made up of grunts and squeals. Gamorreans are not technologically advanced and are known throughout the galaxy as little more than thugs.

CULTURE

Gamorreans live in clans ruled by a Clan Matron. The Clan Matron chooses a Warlord to rule alongside her based on his strength and skills in combat. The female of the species' main job is farming. Gamorr is covered in forests, but the Gamorreans chop down the trees to clear the land for harvesting. The males are employed in hunting and waging wars against rival clans. War is seen as glorious, and violent clashes are rife on Gamorr. Gamorrean technology and weapons are primitive. They prefer axes and lances to blasters and are unlikely to have discovered space travel by themselves.

GAMORREANS IN THE GALAXY

Their brutish nature made Gamorreans ideal mercenaries, guards, and henchmen. Gartogg and Jubnuk were just two of the many Gamorreans the crime lord Jabba the Hutt employed to enforce his rule in his palace on Tatooine. They were not clever but thuggish, so were imposing to Jabba's visitors and a reminder of his strength.

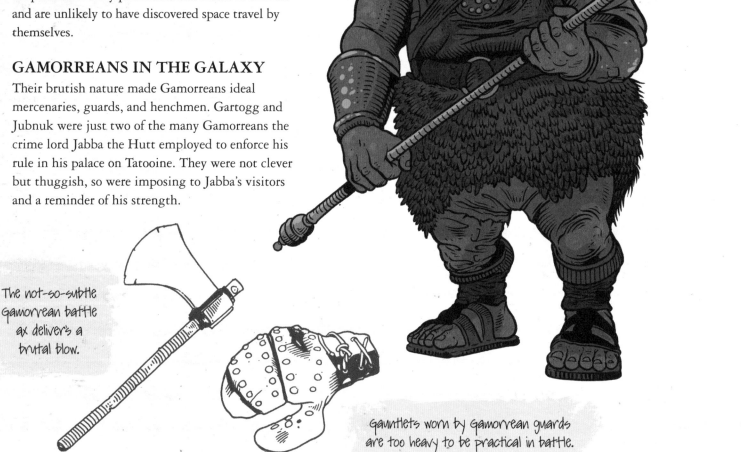

The not-so-subtle Gamorrean battle ax delivers a brutal blow.

Gauntlets worn by Gamorrean guards are too heavy to be practical in battle.

↓フ𝖪ↆフ𝗈∨Ξ𝖪ↆ

TRANDOSHAN

HOMEWORLD: TRANDOSHA

Trandoshans are large, reptilian humanoids with long claws and powerful limbs, perfect for climbing trees in the thick jungles of their home planet. They are renowned across the galaxy for their excellent hunting skills. With quick reflexes, modified weaponry, and natural agility, Trandoshans move on their prey with ruthless precision.

CULTURE

Trandoshans love the thrill of the hunt more than anything else, and a young member's first hunt is seen as a rite of passage in Trandoshan society. Many made careers in game and bounty hunting, and were merciless in pursuing their targets. The Trandoshans had control of the moon Wasskah, which they used as a big game reserve. The hunter Garnac ran a hunting guild that kidnapped other sentient beings from across the galaxy and released them on Wasskah, inviting Trandoshans to come and hunt for sport. Trandoshans have a fierce rivalry with Wookiees, whose home planet neighbors Trandosha in the Kashyyyk system. Wookiees were a particularly popular prey, but in trying to bring more of the hairy giants to his reserve, Garnac met with his demise. Wookiee reinforcements invaded, and Garnac was thrown to his death.

The Hound's Tooth: the famed bounty hunter Bossk's ship.

TRANDOSHANS IN THE GALAXY

Bossk was one of the most notorious bounty hunters in the galaxy during the Galactic Empire. He followed in the footsteps of his father, who taught him how to steal a landspeeder and also passed on his hatred of Wookiees. Bossk was known far and wide for his fearsome skills in killing this rival species. The bounty hunter gained many jobs tracking, capturing, and blackmailing the enemies of crime lords and tyrants, including competing with other bounty hunters to track down the *Millennium Falcon* for Darth Vader and the Empire.

ᗡᔕᔕᑲᑎ GRAN

HOMEWORLD: MALASTARE

Gran are a three-eyed species with antennae atop their heads. A sociable and peaceful people, the Gran live peacefully alongside the Dug on their home planet of Malastare. The Dug control the planet's natural fuel reserves, but the Gran are the ruling species, representing the whole planet at the Galactic Senate. Their diplomatic and peaceable nature makes the Gran ideal ambassadors and negotiators. Mawhonic, a Gran podracer, has the advantage of being able to see more of the light spectrum than most of his opponents. Ree-Yees worked for Jabba looking after his pet frog-dog.

Jabba's pet had a miserable-looking keeper.

FROG-DOG

HOMEWORLD: UNKNOWN

Frog-dogs are clever, sentient beings despite being regularly mistaken for vermin. They use this fact to their advantage and allow prosperous masters to keep them as pets so they have a constant supply of food and shelter. These ugly little beasts are often ignored and can therefore sneak unnoticed into palaces or ships and complete secretive tasks. Jabba the Hutt kept a frog-dog called Buboicullaar as a pet in his palace. The crime lord's guests overlooked Bubo as an unintelligent pest, but the frog-dog actually protected Jabba from many assassination attempts.

Jabba was surrounded by servants and pets. The frog-dog acted as a guard and growled at anyone who approached.

ᚲᚾᛖᚲᚤᚾᚲᚹ
ASKAJIAN

HOMEWORLD: ASKAJI

Askajians are sentient humanoids that live in tribes led by a chief. Yarna d'al' Gargan was the daughter of one such chief, and on her homeworld of Askaji would use her love of dance to honor her tribe. When slavers captured her and transported her to Jabba's palace, Gargan was made to entertain the crime lord with her dancing skills instead.

A Gand bounty hunter was on the lookout for his next job. He was bragging about his exceptional tracking skills.

ᛇᚲᚾᚠ
GAND

HOMEWORLD: GAND

Gands are used to an ammonia-rich atmosphere on their home planet and require breathing equipment when traveling offworld. Some Gands are almost supernaturally gifted at tracking. These members are called findsmen and practice a mystical Gand tradition. Zuckuss was the first findsman to leave Gand, and he became a successful bounty hunter.

ᔑᔑᔑ (Aurebesh: JAKKU)

JAKKU

I have heard tales of the ship graveyard on Jakku for years. At the very end of the Empire's reign over the galaxy, a great battle took place in the skies over the desert planet and left the wrecks of once magnificent vessels lodged in the sand. When I visited, I realized a whole culture had appeared around the fallen ships, drawing in life on an otherwise barren world.

I landed my ship at an outpost buzzing with scavengers and traders. So many different creatures bustled around me, hauling scrap, haggling with vendors, and washing their finds at the large troughs. A crolute barked menacingly at a rival merchant from behind a market stall.

I ventured out into the desert to see the fallen Star Destroyer I had heard so much about and was shocked as the mammoth ship rose out of the dunes in front of me. A Nu-cosian scavenger with an unusual selection of items and creatures on his back ambled past me, and several humans wrapped in protective gear searched the area for useful parts. I knew the storms here could be deadly, so I kept a close eye on the sky.

As the day grew darker and the wind picked up, it was time to seek shelter. I was just turning back toward the outpost when a pair of red eyes popped up out of the sand. I was not interested in becoming a snack for the desert nightlife, so I quickly made my escape. . . .

ꓘꓱꓦꓞꓵꓥꓞꓓ

ABEDNEDO

HOMEWORLD: ABEDNEDO

Abednedos are sentient humanoids who are naturally curious and tolerant of other species. They are able to adapt to different cultures and learn many languages. They are seen as a gregarious and clever species, with their own language and writing system. The Empire's occupation of their home planet inspired many Abednedos to join the rebellion against it.

CULTURE

Abednedos evolved from a species that lived in warrens underground. Eventually Abednedos began to live on the surface of their planet, building multiple cities for the growing population. To an outsider these cities seem chaotic and ostentatious, but for the Abednedos their world is filled with amusement and color.

ABEDNEDOS IN THE GALAXY

This commonly seen species is found on multiple worlds and in many professions. Some represented their planet in the Galactic and New Republic Senates. Others turned to a life of crime, trading in stolen armor and spare parts. Many allied themselves with the rebel cause and then with the Resistance. Ello Asty, for example, was a member of the New Republic's precision air team prior to joining the Resistance. He was a superb pilot but was prone to reckless behavior. He died during the attack on Starkiller Base. His fellow Abednedo C'ai Threnalli flew as Commander Poe Dameron's wingman and remained loyal to him when he mutinied against Admiral Holdo.

Here on Jakku I met a notable Abednedo, a scavenger called Crusher Roodown. When his boss, Unkar Plutt, thought he was selling salvage to another junk dealer, he had Roodown's arms cut off and replaced with load-lifting mechanical arms. These greatly increased his strength and made him an unmissable sight.

CROLUTE

HOMEWORLD: CRUL

Crolutes are an exclusively male species; their female counterparts are called Gilliands. They are gargantuan and aquatic, with buoyant skin and flipper-like feet. Both the male and female species hail from a planet in the Mid Rim territories covered in shallow seas and lagoons. Despite being away from the salt water of their homeworld, traveling Crolutes maintain their gelatinous appearance.

CROLUTES IN THE GALAXY

Unkar Plutt, a Crolute junk trader, made his living on the planet Jakku. He bought weapons, ship parts, and scrap from local scavengers and visitors at his stall at the Niima Outpost, and was known for driving a hard bargain. This ruthless Crolute hired thugs to enforce his stranglehold near the settlement.

What an aquatic life-form was doing on an arid planet is baffling, but this Crolute had a tight grip on all the comings and goings at this desert outpost. He had a group of threatening henchmen who were on the lookout for any scavengers not abiding by the Crolute's rules and were not shy about waving their blasters around. They had their faces covered for anonymity, padded gloves, and glare-blocking goggles.

complete facial coverings were common in the harsh climate on Jakku. Not being able to identify anyone did make it seem like everyone was up to no good though.

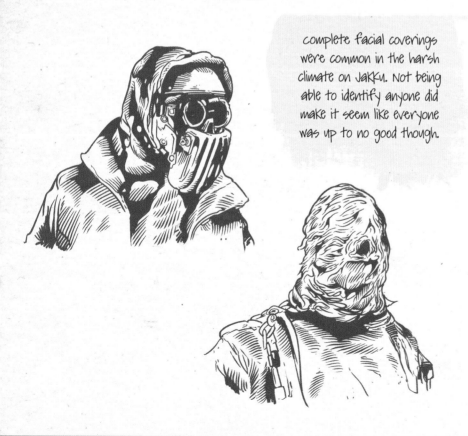

ᑐᐯᑕᗡᗧ

KYUZO

HOMEWORLD: PHATRONG

Kyuzo are sentient humanoids with yellow eyes who are widely traveled across the galaxy. As a species they are instilled with a strong sense of justice and frequently pursue careers in law enforcement. They are famed for their excellence in combat and have a proud martial history on their homeworld of Phatrong.

UNUSUAL PHYSICALITY

The gravity on Phatrong is a lot heavier than average, and because of this Kyuzo have evolved superior muscle strength and fast reflexes. They are petite and thin, thus concealing their unusual strength and making Kyuzo dangerous opponents to those from standard-gravity worlds. The uncommon atmosphere of Phatrong also means that Kyuzo have to protect their eyes and use masks or scarves to cover their faces when on foreign planets. Their sensitive vision and respiratory systems lead to illness when exposed to other atmospheres for too long.

CULTURE

Kyuzo believe oaths and contracts are unbreakable. Their honor and sense of justice are the most important elements in their society and influence many members to take up professions in law enforcement, but also as bounty hunters and mercenaries. Kyuzo form clovocs—organizations of warriors that maintain law and order in the different regions of their homeworld. These warriors traditionally wear wide-brimmed hats that not only protect them from Phatrong's monsoon season but also can be used as shields or weapons in combat.

KYUZO IN THE GALAXY

On Jakku, a constable named Zuvio patrolled the Niima Outpost with his fellow Kyuzo deputies, Drego and Streehn. Jakku was full of crooks trying to take advantage of their fellow settlers. Most believed money was all they needed to get their way, but because of his ingrained Kyuzo honor code, Zuvio could not be bribed. Embo was a Kyuzo bounty hunter during the Clone Wars, taking jobs notably for Boba Fett and the Grand Hutt Council.

BLARINA

HOMEWORLD: CONA

The Blarina are known for being short and very clever. They are infamous liars and can often get themselves out of any scrapes through their love of language. Their broad faces all look much the same to non-Blarina, so it is very hard for outsiders to tell one member of the species from another. They are quick-witted and therefore able to lie extremely convincingly in almost any situation. They aren't known for being particularly hospitable to other species and delight in playing tricks. Blarina stick together and form family-based organizations for dealing with larger species.

Every Blarina I have met has been highly sociable, with a fondness for words. They love to chat, but their Basic only really covers sarcasm.

A modified sorosuub JSP-14 pistol

MELITTO

HOMEWORLD: LI-TORAN

Melittos are insectile humanoids with no eyes or mouths. They are able to sense their environment through the supersensitive hairs on their bodies. They also have a keen sense of smell, which helps them navigate and track. Similar, to the Dybrinthe, Melittos can only breathe in certain atmospheres and have to wear breathing equipment on foreign planets. In Melitto society, individuals live in hives ruled by a queen, whose position is gained through combat. Sarco Plank was a revered Melitto bounty hunter. He notably once dueled with Luke Skywalker while working as a tomb raider on the planet Devaron, and years later could be found on Jakku making a living through scavenging.

꓄ꓦꓱꓶꓲꙡꓶꓴꓱꙡ

DYBRINTHE

HOMEWORLD: DYBRIN 12

Dybrinthe are a humanoid species with bright skin and a gill-like respiratory system. This is not suited to travel off their homeworld, so they are required to wear breathing apparatus in other climates. Dybrinthe live in clans, with vicious conflicts between them over territories and fuel. Rival clan members tunnel underground and attempt to divert fuel to their own territories. It is unusual to see Dybrinthe who have left Dybrin 12, but one notable exception was Athgar Hecce. Hecce was a bounty hunter who visited Jakku during the cold war and found its climate cool and pleasant after operating in higher-atmospheric environments.

ꓵꓴ–ꙡꓳꙡꓲꓘꓵ

NU-COSIAN

HOMEWORLD: COSIAN SPACE

Nu-Cosians are a genetically engineered race of the Cosian species. Cosians are reptilian humanoids with long tails and mottled green skin. Nu-Cosians have longer necks, and their tails are strong and help with balance and even self-defense. Bobbajo, a male Nu-Cosian, was known as the Crittermonger on Jakku, because he could be seen carrying around cages full of small animals. Some he sold to spacers as food, but others were thought to be kept as his pets. He was a great storyteller, though few of his tales could be believed, and his calming voice settled the creatures living on his back.

Bobbajo showed me the curious creatures in his cage. He talks to these lively sneeps like old friends.

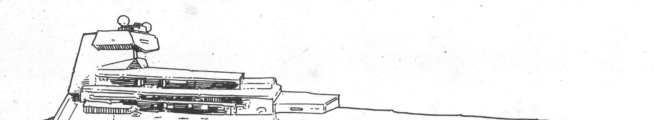

JEDHA

I had always been fascinated by the legends surrounding Jedha. Many believed it held the secrets to the origins of the Jedi order, and many spiritual pilgrims journeyed to its Holy City. This sandy city was full of ancient architecture and surrounded by a large wall.

The Temple of the Kyber came into view as I entered the city. The streets were dotted with the simple red robes of the Disciples of the Whills, the Force-worshipping followers of Jedha's oldest faith—not to be confused with the Guardians of the Whills, the order of warrior monks who protected the temple and all who visited it.

Many species traveled to Jedha, some religious, some decisively not. As I strolled through the port I came across an Anomid in traditional robes, making her way to the temple. A blue-skinned bounty hunter crossed my path in search of his target. Members of a dissident gang made deals in the corner.

ANOMID

HOMEWORLD: YABLARI

This sentient species with their recognizable masks are often seen throughout the galaxy. It is a common misconception that the masks are breathing filters, but they are actually vocoder masks, which enable speech. Anomids have no vocal cords, so they communicate with each other through sign language and body language. The vocoder masks are able to translate their utterings into speech that other species can then understand.

In the Holy city I recognized an Anomid. Though she was concealed by the red robes of the Guardians of the Whills, her vocoder gave away her origins.

I wonder why the Britarro are such a mysterious species. Not much is known about their origins.

BRITARRO

HOMEWORLD: BRITAXIS MINOR

A rather notorious member of this humanoid species is one Nik Hepho, a bounty hunter who specializes in hunting down those suspected of following the outlawed religion known as the Church of the Force. With unmistakable smooth blue skin, he is not an easy character to miss.

ꝺꝺꞑꞗ꞊ꞗ꞉ꞇꞑ DRABATAN

HOMEWORLD: PIPADA

Drabatans are amphibious humanoids whose homeworld has been harvested for materials by the Empire, displacing much of the native population. Pao was a notable Drabatan who served as a commando for the rebel forces during the Battle of Scarif. Drabatans are freshwater amphibiods, so the salt water on Scarif was unpleasant for Pao. He nevertheless charged into battle with his Drabatese war cry of *"Sa'kalla!"* against his Imperial enemies, inspiring his many squad mates to follow suit. There is a skilled Drabatan mechanic on staff at the Resistance base on D'Qar.

ꞇꞑꞅ꞊ꞇꞇꞑ MEFTIAN

HOMEWORLD: UNKNOWN

This sentient, fur-covered species is humanoid in build. With long black-and-white fur, the Meftians are slightly reminiscent of that other famed woolly species, the Wookiees. Kullbee Sperado was a gunslinger in Gerrera's gang.

saw Gerrera is known to be charismatic but ruthless.

Here on Jedha I have heard many stories of a rebel group called the Partisans. Led by a human named Saw Gerrera, this alliance seeks to destabilize the Imperial occupation, but their violent methods are not always appreciated by the locals.

KEREDIAN

HOMEWORLD: UNKNOWN

Little is known of this sentient humanoid species, including their homeworld. Cycyed Ock, a member of Saw Gerrera's rebel cell on Jedha, was large, green, and had a cyberoptic wire attached to his brain to enhance his vision. He carried a Keredian vibrorang, which was a boomerang-like weapon.

GIGORAN

HOMEWORLD: GIGOR

These sentient, tall, hairy humanoids are often enslaved for their strength. Indeed, the role of bodyguard is a common occupation among this species. Perhaps the most famed of this usually peaceful species is Moroff, a Gigoran mercenary who sells his skills to the highest bidder, regardless of political allegiance. He became an outlaw as a member of Saw Gerrera's rebel cell on Jedha during the Imperial occupation. Due to their powerful strength, many Gigorans were enslaved on Kessel to work the spice mines.

ᒡᔗ↙ᒍ◌1ᐱ1

TALPINI

HOMEWORLD: TAL PI

Thanks to their smaller stature, these diminutive humanoids can conceal themselves easily among taller beings—particularly useful when operating in clandestine circumstances. Weeteef Cyu-Bee was one such Talpini who exploited his build while a member of Saw Gerrera's rebels on Jedha.

↙ᒃᓭᒃ↙

SABAT

HOMEWORLD: UNKNOWN

A humanoid species with a recognizable low forehead and elongated, cone-shaped cranium, they have tufty hair that grows around the sides and on top of the skull. The Sabat known as Leevan Tenza made a name for himself by aligning with Saw Gerrera after being court-martialed by General Dodonna's team of rebels for disobeying orders. A male Sabat named Gelan Yees was a member of Enfys Nest's gang.

The Partisans' emblem, often worn by Saw Gerrera, originated during the clone wars among Onderon rebels.

Saw Gerrera's gang is made up of many different species, all with mysterious backgrounds— a fascinating group.

ᚤᚖᚋᚄᚔᚍ VOBATI

HOMEWORLD: VOBES

A little-known species, the Vobati have carved out niches for themselves throughout the galaxy. There are tales of one famed Vobati named Valwid Ined—an inhabitant of Jedha during the Imperial occupation. He worked as a forger, supplying Saw's gang with counterfeit transit visas to get past Imperial checkpoints.

ᚋᚔᚐᚋᚔᚍ MAIRAN

HOMEWORLD: MAIRES

Also referred to as Bors, this multipod creature is said to have the ability to read minds. It uses its vast body to entrap its victim and attaches its tentacles to their temples. Saw Gerrera kept a Mairan, Bor Gullet, in his hideout to torture and extract information from his prisoners. Bodhi Rook, a deserting Imperial pilot, almost lost his mind following his interrogation.

I think I remember Bor Gullet. . . .

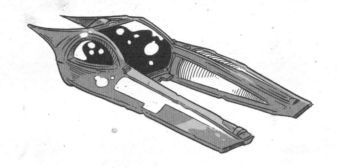

ᚺᚱᚢᚱᚢᚢᚱᚱᚷᚢ

CORUSCANT

Coruscant, one of the most influential planets in the galaxy, is home to two of the most powerful organizations: the Galactic Senate and the Jedi Order. Visiting this cosmopolitan hub in the heart of the core worlds, I discovered a vibrant culture of trade and industry. Coruscant draws creatures from all over looking for work, entertainment, and political enrichment.

I stared up at Coruscant's Galactic City, filled with towering skyscrapers reaching at least six thousands meters up into the atmosphere. I traveled through the city's various sectors, including the financial district full of businesses and banks, some residential zones, and the all-important federal sector where the Senate and Jedi Order reside. Airspeeders whizzed past my head through skytunnels along preprogrammed routes. This hive of industriousness was well organized, protected, and monitored.

While on Coruscant I visited its two most famous buildings: the Senate Rotunda and the Jedi Temple. Here I found aliens of all affiliations. I watched a very clever Siniteen argue for his planet's well-being while the lesser-known Tarnab species grumbled in the corner. The Jedi Temple brought together empathetic Nautolans and easily offended Roonans, all practicing mystical Force skills in harmony.

GALACTIC SENATE

During my time on Coruscant, I visited the senate Rotunda to watch a political debate. This was an immense building with a chamber filled with seats on circular platforms called hoverpods. When a member wished to speak, the hoverpod they were seated on would detach from the wall and float to the center of the chamber.

Species from all over the galaxy send representatives to discuss legislation, with over a thousand members in attendance. At the center of the chamber the supreme chancellor and the vice chair preside over the meetings from their podium. Like the other platforms, this was equipped with a translation device that allowed the many different dialects to be understood.

CHAGRIAN

HOMEWORLD: CONA

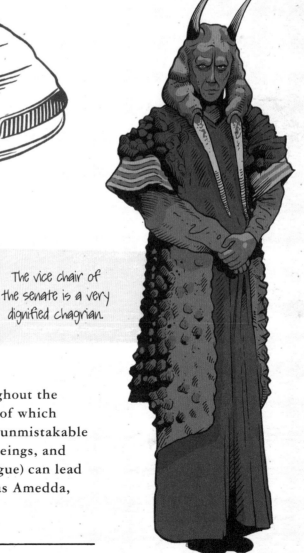

The vice chair of the senate is a very dignified chagrian.

These blue-skinned, amphibious bipeds are frequently seen throughout the galaxy and are easily identifiable by their two pairs of horns—one of which grows from the skull while the secondary pair protrudes from the unmistakable tails of flesh that grow over their shoulders. They are intelligent beings, and their intimidating appearance (including a long, black, forked tongue) can lead to them holding influential positions of power—like the famed Mas Amedda, who served as Emperor Palpatine's grand vizier.

PANTORAN

ᴏᴋᴀᴊᴏ7ᴋᴀ

HOMEWORLD: PANTORA

The humanoid, blue-skinned Pantorans enjoy the finer things in life with a culture that is extremely sophisticated. They wear beautiful clothing and elegant jewelry, and their golden facial tattoos symbolize their status in society. They are fair and have an uncompromising notion of what is right. They are not afraid to fight for what they believe in, as Chairman Papanoida demonstrated when he took it upon himself to rescue his children after they were kidnapped.

The senator from Kooriva spun away from the wall to address the chancellor. He was striking to observe, with a curious horn atop his head.

KOORIVAR

ᴊᴏᴏ71Yᴋ7

HOMEWORLD: KOORIVA

This is a shrewd species of tall near-humans whose appearance is dominated by a large horn that spirals upward from the center of their heads. They also have smaller horns surrounding it and reptilian skin that can be of many different colors. It's believed that the horn is a status symbol in Koorivian society, with the larger horn denoting a higher class. Koorivars are excellent at reading body language, which has made them skilled businesspeople, like the famed magistrate Passel Argente of the Corporate Alliance.

↓ᴋ⅂ᴧᴋⵚ
TARNAB

HOMEWORLD: TARN

Perhaps the most famed of this mysterious sentient species is Senator Mot-Not Rab, who represented the Tarnab in the Galactic Senate during the Clone Wars. They can be identified by their triangular-shaped skulls and a cluster of horns amid often long hair. They have an elongated snout/nose and black-brown leathery skin.

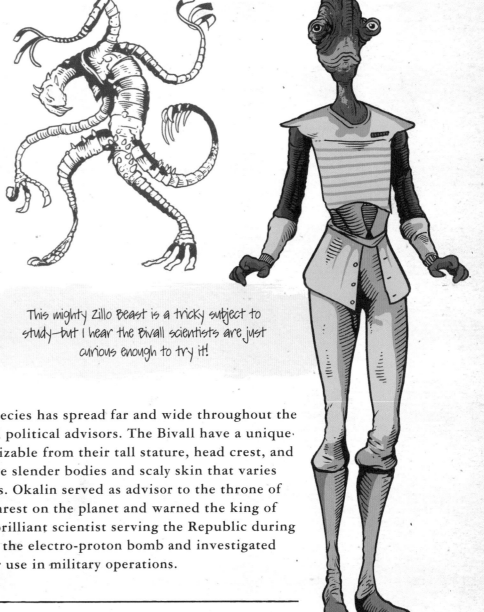

This mighty Zillo Beast is a tricky subject to study—but I hear the Bivall scientists are just curious enough to try it!

 ⵚ⅂ᴧᴋᴧᴧ
BIVALL

HOMEWORLD: PROTOBRANCH

Renowned for their high intelligence, this species has spread far and wide throughout the galaxy as doctors, researchers, scientists, and political advisors. The Bivall have a unique physical appearance and are instantly recognizable from their tall stature, head crest, and large, slightly protruding eyes. They also have slender bodies and scaly skin that varies in color from white to green and many others. Okalin served as advisor to the throne of Onderon. He carefully monitored the civil unrest on the planet and warned the king of any attempts on his life. Sionver Boll was a brilliant scientist serving the Republic during the Clone Wars. She designed and developed the electro-proton bomb and investigated the impenetrable scales of the Zillo Beast for use in military operations.

NEIMOIDIAN

HOMEWORLD: NEIMOIDIA

This green-skinned humanoid species has exceptional business skills and was at one time responsible for building the largest commercial corporation in the galaxy (the infamous Trade Federation)—but they are also deceitful, cowardly, and greedy, driven by wealth and material possessions. Neimoidians are physically similar to the Duros, being tall and thin with red eyes, thin mouths, and no noses. Their greed is cultivated from birth, as they are raised as grubs in communal hives until the age of seven, where they are given limited amounts of food—encouraging a survival-of-the-fittest mentality among them. Perhaps the most famous of their species was Nute Gunray—the treacherous viceroy who instigated the blockade of Naboo.

> The Neimoidians seem extremely arrogant and lazy to me. They are business savvy, but it seems they will not perform a task themselves if they can find someone else to do it for them. . . .

KEL DOR

HOMEWORLD: DORIN

A sentient, humanoid species, the Kel Dor are easily recognizable by the specialized breathing apparatus they wear to be able to function in oxygen-rich atmospheres. These masks filter out oxygen, which is poisonous to them, and instead filter in a helium mixture unique to their world. They also wear dark, close-fitting goggles that prevent their eye fluids from evaporating. With their thick peach-pink skin, they have been referred to as an unattractive species—no matter, as they are certainly well respected. Famed Kel Dor Plo Koon was a brave Jedi Master and one of the most powerful Jedi ever.

SINITEEN

HOMEWORLD: MILEVA

This amazing species demonstrates levels of hyperintelligence—most notably their ability to calculate hyperspace jumps without the aid of a computer! With their pale skin, pupilless eyes, and veiny, oversized heads, they must have large and advanced brains to be able to perform these types of calculations. It's no wonder that Pons Limbic, a Siniteen who frequented the Mos Eisley cantina, was nicknamed Brainiac.

Are these really the most intelligent humanoids in the galaxy?

Two Anx stood behind me engaged in conversation. Their deep, rumbling voices vibrated through me. I've never heard anything like it!

ANX

HOMEWORLD: GRAVLEX MED

This extremely tall, reptilian, sentient species was well regarded during the time of the Galactic Senate and the Jedi Order—two organizations in which they had representatives (although Force-sensitive Anx are rare). Anx are instantly recognizable from their blade-shaped head, which features a crest that changes color according to each individual's mood. They also have a hunched stature that, along with their low voice, is a direct result of the atmosphere on their homeworld, which has higher-than-average gravity.

ᒍᐺᓇᔥᔕ ᔕᐺᓇᒪᐺᒪ

JEDI TEMPLE

The Jedi Order is answerable to the Republic and therefore has had to build its headquarters in the same city as the seat of government. The Jedi Temple on Coruscant is a sight to behold. As I climbed the ceremonial staircase to the entrance, I noted the imposing pylons adorned with depictions of the founding Masters.

The vast interior was full of corridors leading to shrines, where Jedi Knights reflected on the will of the Force. I followed my guide deeper into the temple, where we passed a training center for younglings. These Force-sensitive children of all species practiced their skills alongside Jedi Masters in the hope of becoming Knights of the order.

I was not permitted to enter the chamber where the Jedi High council sat. It was described as a circular room in one of the four towers where the Masters of the day met to discuss the affairs of the Jedi. The council swore allegiance to the Republic, but they had complete autonomy over the governing of the Jedi order.

The Force is an energy binding the galaxy together. Those sensitive to it can sometimes use its power for telekinesis and mind control, but it can also give them advanced reflexes and combat skills. The Jedi Order invites those with extreme sensitivity to the Force to join them in the defense of the galaxy. Jedi Masters have the ability to sense great evil through the Force to alert them to conflict.

The midi-chlorians (microscopic life-forms inside all organisms) in an individual's blood determine how connected to the Force they are. Rumor has it that Anakin Skywalker had more midi-chlorians than any Jedi ever tested.

FORCE-WIELDERS

HOMEWORLD: MORTIS

Force-wielders have no fixed form, so they can look like any species they choose. They are highly intelligent and have such an affinity with the Force that they were believed by some to be gods. A family of Force-wielders lived on Mortis, rumored to be where the Force originated. The family was made up of the Son, who was aligned with the dark side of the Force; the Daughter, who was aligned with the light; and the Father, who kept the balance between them.

ᔏᗱᒍᗱᐁᗱᔕ

UNKNOWN

HOMEWORLD: UNKNOWN

Yoda, one of the greatest-known Jedi, was a member of a mysterious species with no known name or home planet. Information is hard to come by due to their ancient and secretive nature. Yaddle, a fellow Jedi Master, was the only other known member of this species. Yoda was strong with the light side of the Force and trained many generations of Jedi.

Perhaps whatever species Yoda belongs to is naturally strong with the Force. Both he and Yaddle are greatly revered here in the Jedi Temple.

JEDI MASTER

Despite his small size and aged appearance, Yoda was extremely proficient in many Jedi powers. He could jump many feet into the air, move heavy objects with his mind, sense disturbances from miles away, and also deflect other Force powers directed against him. He was considered to be one of the most skilled users of the lightsaber in the whole Order, being quick, agile, and fearless in combat.

Yaddle is known for being very kind and quiet, but on the other hand possesses some of the deadliest Force powers.

Yoda was born nearly nine hundred years before the Battle of Yavin and died not long after. His extremely long life had an impact on many galactic events. Rising to the highest position in the Order, this Grand Master oversaw the Jedi High Council and was relied on for his great wisdom and experience. He taught Jedi younglings lightsaber skills and decided who should be let into the Order.

During the era of the Republic, Yoda reluctantly allowed a young boy named Anakin Skywalker to be trained as a Padawan by Jedi Knight Obi-Wan Kenobi. Anakin grew up to be a great Jedi, but was seduced to the dark side of the Force. He became one of the most dangerous Sith Lords of all time, Darth Vader. When Vader's new master Darth Sidious ordered the death of all Jedi, Yoda was forced to flee.

Yoda spent his exile on the swamp planet Dagobah. It was here he met Anakin's son, Luke, who became Yoda's final trainee. Yoda taught Luke the ways of the Force and encouraged him to reject the dark side. Luke was present at Yoda's death, where the Master told the young Jedi that his training was complete.

But death was not the end for Yoda. He learned from the spirit of Qui-Gon Jinn that it was possible for a Jedi's essence to survive beyond death if they completed a secret course of training. Yoda's Force ghost appeared to Luke Skywalker many times, including when he set him on the right course when he was conflicted about the future of the Jedi.

Although I was not allowed in the council chamber, a young Padawan hoping to become a Jedi Knight told me all about the ring of chairs filled with the greatest Jedi alive. . . .

MIKKIAN

HOMEWORLD: MIKKIA

Little is known about this mysterious humanoid species. However, perhaps their most distinguishing feature is their long head-tendrils, which seem to differ greatly between individuals. The Mikkians have amazing skin pigmentation, which seems to incorporate an entire spectrum of beautiful, vivid colors, including blue, green, yellow, and pink. Two notable Mikkians are twin sisters Tiplar and Tiplee, who were both Jedi Knights killed during the Clone Wars.

Kit Fisto is a well-respected Jedi Master who loves to crack a joke!

NAUTOLAN

HOMEWORLD: GLEE ANSELM

Nautolans have trademark long tentacles hanging from their heads that are not just for show but are actually able to detect different chemical signatures. This allows Nautolans to gauge the subconscious emotions of others. An amphibious species, Nautolans live both on land and in water. They are extremely strong swimmers, and their striking large black eyes are adapted for vision in low-lit underwater conditions. The celebrated Jedi Kit Fisto was a famed Nautolan.

ONGREE

HOMEWORLD: SKUSTELL

These sentient amphibians often give the impression that their heads are on upside down due to the curious positioning of their facial features and long, tapered cranium. Among their many curious physical attributes are two eyestalks, which emerge from either side of the head, and a lipless mouth placed in the center of their forehead above four nostrils. Despite their unconventional looks, many Ongree are considered to be even-minded individuals and can be found as diplomats and negotiators throughout the galaxy. There are several Ongree who have become Jedi, including the brave Jedi Knight Pablo-Jill and Jedi Master Coleman Kcaj.

The piscine Jedi with the upside-down features looked fearsome!

QUERMIAN

HOMEWORLD: QUERMIA

The curious appearance of this sentient species is almost a match for their even more curious physiology. They have long limbs and an extremely extended neck but, remarkably, no spine, which affords them a vast array of movements that many other species would find impossible to perform. They have two pairs of arms, the second of which is often kept concealed beneath garments. They also have two brains: an upper, which is located in the head, and a lower, which is positioned inside the chest. They have no nose on their face but instead smell with glands in their hands. The respected Jedi Master Yarael Poof was a Quermian.

BESALISK

HOMEWORLD: OJOM

I stopped off at an eatery, which seemed very popular with the locals. The owner had a friendly nature and told many tales of adventure. His four arms allowed him to prepare food nonstop!

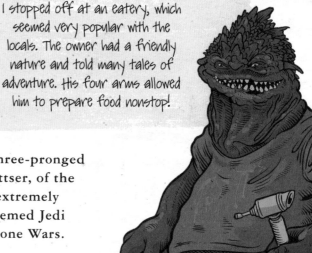

Besalisks are industrious humanoids with four arms, three-pronged head crests, and an inflatable wattle. While Dexster Jettser, of the Coruscant establishment Dex's Diner, was considered extremely friendly and likeable, not all Besalisks are so nice. Esteemed Jedi Master Pong Krell was a ruthless general during the Clone Wars.

Pong Krell wielded two double-bladed lightsabers at the same time! A formidable opponent on the battlefield.

VURK

The Vurk are not a common sight around the temple. I believe only one of the species has ever been known to join the Jedi Order.

HOMEWORLD: SEMBLA

A species of tall reptilian humanoids, the Vurk can be identified by the prominent and bony crests sitting atop their heads. The head crest is a key feature of the species and continues to grow throughout the life of the Vurk. They have thick reptilian skin, which is green. For some reason, it is commonly thought that the Vurk are a primitive species, but they are actually highly empathetic and skilled mediators. The Vurk Coleman Trebor was one of the few of his species to join the Jedi Order.

THOLOTHIAN

HOMEWORLD: THOLOTH

Little is known about this seemingly ageless species, but the celebrated Jedi Master Adi Gallia was Tholothian. These sentient humanoids have scaled craniums and can be identified by the long, fleshy white tendrils that grow from them. Gallia's cousin, Stass Allie, was a Jedi general and led many troopers into battle during the Clone Wars.

ROONAN

HOMEWORLD: ROONA

The Roonans' skin color is blue-gray, and they have a ridged forehead and cranium with large, almond-shaped blue eyes. Short in stature, they have big ideas and are notoriously easy to offend. They have been known to take even the slightest slipup as a deep insult. It is also rumored that they have tiny teeth, but it would be a mistake to question them on it. Jedi Master Halsey was of this species.

CEREAN

HOMEWORLD: CEREA

I observed the Jedi Master from Cerea teaching Makashi, a very elegant lightsaber-wielding technique.

This striking-looking humanoid species is easily identified by their enlarged, cone-shaped cranium that houses an incredibly complex brain. Cereans are believed to have great thinking capabilities. The impressive brain of a Cerean is binary, meaning that it is able to process many things at the same time, sort through data quickly, and also consider two sides of the same argument simultaneously. They also possess two hearts—the second of which works to supply extra blood and oxygen to their brain. Ki-Adi-Mundi was a Cerean Jedi Master and member of the Jedi High Council.

ᚹᚳᚾᛏᚢ ᚾᛏᚥᚹᚹᛏᚢ

CITY STREETS

coruscant is a metropolitan world filled with nightclubs, diners, and cantinas, but the city is also home to a criminal underworld. Thieves, dealers, and members of other shady professions thrive here among the tourists and political visitors. I had to keep an eye on my possessions and avoid the dark alleys throughout the city.

A horned alien recommended the Almakian desserts at a nearby diner. The pie was out of this world!

ᚹᚢᚳᚳᚨᚾᛚᚥᚨᚢᚷ

LEFFINGITE

HOMEWORLD: ALMAK

This orange-skinned, four-eyed, horn-headed sentient species found themselves under attack from the government after the rise of the Galactic Empire, and many were forced to flee their homeworld. Like the petty criminal Magaloof, many found their way to Coruscant, where an Almakian apple pie dish has made its way onto the menu at Dex's Diner.

ISHI TIB

During a walk around the city, I was startled when a leaf started a conversation with me! However, upon closer inspection I realized it was actually an Ishi Tib. . . .

HOMEWORLD: TIBRIN

These friendly, amphibious humanoids have a rather striking appearance with their green skin, almost star-shaped face, beak-like mouth, and large, bulbous gold eyes. They have an excellent sense of smell, both on land and in water, and on their homeworld they have built their cities on coral reefs. As a water-dwelling species, they are very much concerned with ecological preservation, but they are seen throughout the galaxy in a variety of jobs, including within the Rebel Alliance.

clawdites are good at human disguises!

CLAWDITE

HOMEWORLD: ZOLAN

Clawdites are reptilian humanoids whose defining feature is their ability to change shape. They are able to impersonate any humanoid using great concentration and focus. Clawdites are often solitary beings, and those who use their shape-shifting abilities spend their time learning meditation to maximize their abilities. These unique talents make Clawdites ideally suited to professions such as spying, bounty hunting, and military service. Zam Wessell was a female Clawdite bounty hunter before the Clone Wars. She was a frequent accomplice of Jango Fett and was once hired by him to assassinate Senator Padmé Amidala. Jedi Knights Obi-Wan Kenobi and Anakin Skywalker foiled her attempt, resulting in Jango's decision to silence Zam instead.

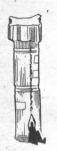

GEONOSIS

Geonosis is an arid planet with red across the sky and land as far as the eye can see. It is covered in hive spires filled with industrial pursuits of the winged natives. There is not much to recommend this mostly uninhabitable world, but there was one sight I was longing to witness.

I traveled to Geonosis to satisfy my morbid curiosity about its gladiatorial arena. This dry world in the Outer Rim was home to the Geonosian species, whose famed form of entertainment was to force prisoners into the arena and pit them against ravenous beasts.

I approached the Petranaki arena, named for the gladiatorial beast battles that take place inside. The arena was a large ampitheater with a circular sand pit in the middle for the exhibition. There were balconies for the more affluent attendees, while the rest of us filled the stands.

I took a seat in the hundred-thousand-strong crowd. The refreshment prices were extortionate, but the arena was hot and dusty, so a drink was required. The beasts that emerged were aggressive and gross, but the winged spectators broke into rowdy cheering all around me. This savage pastime was not my cup of tea.

ᐠᗐᗝᐯᐠᐱ

ACKLAY

HOMEWORLD: VENDAXA

This gigantic amphibian is famous as one of the beasts used by the Geonosians in the notorious Petranaki execution arena. With its six lethal claws, razor-sharp teeth, and three eyes, this natural underwater predator still makes for a deadly opponent on land, with a particularly dangerous bite. Thanks to an organ beneath its chin that senses body electricity, the acklay can easily identify its prey, which it then spears with its claws, while its tough, leathery skin affords it much protection. Its naturally aggressive nature makes it a favorite in arenas—as Jedi Knight Obi-Wan Kenobi discovered almost to his cost.

As I sat in the arena with my fellow spectators, watching this gigantic creature scuttling to and fro, I realized this is one species I am happy to observe from a distance.

After seeing this creature in action, I have come to the conclusion that I am not a cat person.

ᎶᏙᏙᏗᎶ

NEXU

HOMEWORLD: CHOLGANNA

Prized for entertainment in combat arenas, this fur-covered feline is a fearsome sight to behold. A natural predator, it combines feline agility with a killer set of teeth and claws, plus two sets of red eyes (which have infrared vision) and sharp quills designed to inflict deadly wounds. While its light build renders it vulnerable to attack, it also makes the nexu quick and deadly. Once caught within these fangs, unfortunate prey is only one bite or shake away from death.

ᒋᏙᏙᎶᏙ

REEK

When I asked a guard why the reek was so angry, he simply laughed. . . .

HOMEWORLD: CODIAN MOON

This imposing-looking creature, with its three horns and powerful jaws, has become a source of sporting entertainment for arena goers. Although reeks are herbivorous, the arena guards starve them until they are mad with hunger, then feed them meat to fuel their aggression. Naturally a grayish-brown color, the red coloring of arena reeks is the result of an enforced meat diet. While their large, heavy build makes them relatively slow-moving, they are nevertheless dangerous. They can gore opponents and go head to head with other reeks.

ᎶᏍᏍᏦᏙ

ORRAY

HOMEWORLD: GEONOSIS

Orrays are large, sturdy quadrupeds with long snouts and impressive strength. They are very popular with Geonosians as they can perform multiple tasks in the arena. In the wild these creatures have long stinger tails, but the Geonosians remove them to easily domesticate the orrays as mounts and to make them pull carts around the arena.

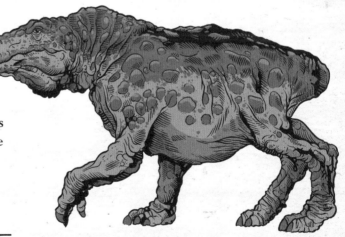

GEONOSIAN

HOMEWORLD: GEONOSIS

Geonosians are a winged species whose most notable contribution to galactic events was the creation of the Separatist droid army. Geonosian entertainment centers on a gladiatorial arena, which host battles for the entertainment of the people and punishment of Geonosian enemies.

CULTURE

Geonosian society is split into hives. Each member belongs to a nest with drones, warriors, and a queen. The queen lays eggs for the hive and provides orders to the government of Geonosis. Drones are the lowest-ranking in the society but can become part of the revered warrior set if they prove themselves in combat. The species is seen as being naturally industrious and productive, and the drones are regularly tasked with building factories and other structures for outside parties. Geonosians celebrate the virtues of the industry of the hives one day a year in a festival called Meckgin. If the hives ever become idle, the warriors become restless, so civil wars are quite common within the hives.

WEAPONS AND TECHNOLOGY

A highly advanced species, Geonosians have superior technology. They perfected sonic weaponry by harnessing sound energy inside a plasma containment charge. They fire this energy with highly destructive sonic blasters, which are the standard weapon of Geonosian soldiers. They also added an electrically charged tip to their beast-herding spears to more effectively tame their creatures and for defense.

Geonosians became loyal to the Confederacy of Independent Systems during the final years of the Republic. Their many underground factories were used to build thousands of battle droids that were then used to fight the Republic's clone army. The battle droids were designed and equipped according to their purpose, including simple weapons for ground combat, pilot programming, advanced technology for commanders, as well as tanks and ships for use on the battlefield.

GEONOSIANS IN THE GALAXY

Poggle the Lesser was the Archduke of Geonosis during the Clone Wars. He oversaw the droid factories and became a key figure in the Confederacy of Independent Systems. Poggle was subservient to the reigning monarch, Queen Karina the Great, but as she stayed underground he became the public leader of the Geonosians. Karina was a frightening figure with an elaborate headdress and six limbs, rather than the usual four. Unfortunately, under the reign of the Emperor, Geonosians were virtually wiped out.

Geonosians called picadors ride orrays in the arena. They use rods to cruelly prod and zap the other beasts to keep them in line.

᚛ᚑᚌᚔᚄ ᚓᚐᚃᚐᚔᚓᚔᚄ᚜

Wet Habitats

Moving away from dusty, dry locations, we turn to those destinations with a lusher landscape. Our traveler explored forests, swamps, and underwater worlds, meeting strange creatures and learning of curious cultures. Humanoid or not, many species thrive on these green worlds.

Forest planets can be beautiful but also scary. Under the dark canopies of Endor, hungry gorax prowl and magical Ewok villages thrive. The jungles are filled with birds, insects, and snakes, and grassy plains attract many herd animals while hiding smaller predators.

Some species evolve gills and fins to live under the water. Gungans build elaborate underwater cities, while the Kaminoans live on top of the ocean surface. The seas of Naboo are filled with beautiful and sometimes dangerous fish, and giant aquatic monsters.

Those creatures that dwell on ice planets are specially equipped to deal with the low temperatures and dangerous terrain. Caves and caverns are ideal shelter on vast snowy plains, and coats of thick fur keep many of these species warm. Watch out, though: these landscapes breed the toughest and most savage predators!

NOGHRI

HOMEWORLD: HONOGHR

The Noghri are gray-skinned with a distinguishing row of horns on their heads. They run on all fours, which enables them to travel quickly without tiring and gives them the ability to jump long distances. They have an excellent sense of smell and are valued for their combat skills, so they are often employed as trackers and assassins.

The Noghri are said to be fearsome warriors. With those sharp teeth and claws I don't doubt it!

OTTEGAN

HOMEWORLD: OTTEGA SYSTEM

Ottegans are genetically similar to Ithorians, and therefore share a similar physiology. However, while Ithorians have two mouths, Ottegans only have one, gaining them the nickname lone mouths, a term used by the Ithorians to mock their cousins. Praster Ommlen was a gunrunner before he joined the Sacred Order of Ramulus, a religion popular among Ithorians.

ZABRAK

HOMEWORLD: IRIDONIA AND DATHOMIR

Iridonian Zabraks are a common sight throughout the galaxy, as they are often drawn to positions that involve travel. Dathomirian Zabraks are seen far less often as they do not trust offworlders. The feared Sith Apprentice Darth Maul was a Dathomirian Zabrak. Iridonian Zabraks are known for their great mental discipline, which allows them to suffer immense physical pain.

EWOK

HOMEWORLD: ENDOR

As I walked through the forest trying to avoid Endor's predators, I discovered a mysterious village in the trees, full of furry creatures who seemed cute, at first. . . .

Ewoks are sentient humanoids, known for their surprising survival skills despite their diminutive stature. They are covered in fur from head to toe but should not be mistaken for cute. A fully grown Ewok is strong enough to overpower combat-trained humans.

CULTURE

The Ewoks are a deeply spiritual people, holding many rituals and festivals with music and celebration. Each community is built on a hierarchy with a chief and council of elders. The most senior members claim the most ornate huts. Despite their isolated and primitive way of life, Ewoks engage in political and artistic pursuits, and communicate in their native language, Ewokese.

HABITAT

Ewoks live in villages built high up in the trees of Endor. Thatched huts connected by a series of rope ladders, bridges, and vines provide housing and social-gathering spaces. The huts are traditionally homely, with a fire in the middle for cooking and warmth. During the summer months some Ewoks stay in fishing villages on the forest floor, making it easier to collect supplies for their storerooms.

PREDATORS

Ewoks use the upper canopies of their villages to keep watch for marauding gorax and flying condor dragons. At night the canopies are illuminated by fires to deter attacks by these giant predators. Unmarried Ewoks keep huts closer to the ground to stand guard against Duloks, who often emerge from the swamps to grab their prey.

TOOLS

The boughs of the trees in Ewok villages are useful for making weapons, tools, and household items. Ewoks use spears, bows, and slingshots to hunt, and larger catapults to defend the colony. They also build hang gliders to quickly travel through the treetops. Though their technology is primitive, Ewoks are quick learners and easily pick up simple mechanical processes.

I spotted many Ewoks working and playing high up in the trees between the thatched huts.

Ewok glider made of animal pelts and wood

EWOKS IN THE GALAXY

Wicket W. Warrick was a member of the Bright Tree Village tribe. He lived an adventurous life with his friends, protecting the village from threats. As a young warrior, Wicket witnessed the Empire's evil up close, when they built a shield generator on Endor to protect the second Death Star. Wicket helped a group of rebels destroy the generator and fight off Imperial troops.

NOSAURIAN

HOMEWORLD: NEW PLYMPTO

Nosaurians are easily recognized by the row of long horns on their heads. As well as being naturally bad-tempered, they often refuse to speak Galactic Basic, instead preferring to communicate in their native language made up of unpleasant hisses and barks. Clegg Holdfast, a male Nosaurian, worked as a journalist for *Podracing Quarterly*, a magazine about Tatooine's most popular and dangerous sport, as well as participating in the races himself.

Two Nosaurians appeared to be having a fight near me, but it turned out barking at each other was just how they communicate.

GORAX

HOMEWORLD: ENDOR

Gorax are giant predators who live in the mountains on a forest moon. They are rarely seen and only leave their habitats to attack Ewok villages for food. They grow to mammoth sizes and have highly sensitive hearing and sharp teeth, perfect for hunting tiny furry creatures, but the Ewoks have a good line of defense. They keep a close watch for marauding gorax through the night and set up traps ideal for bringing down big monsters.

I did not expect to see a gorax during the day, but I must have disturbed one's lair. It didn't have to roar twice before I was running for my life!

AGARIAN

HOMEWORLD: UNKNOWN

It is unknown where this mushroom-like species originated, or even what their true name is. This life-form evolved from fungi and traveled through space as giant seedlings before settling in Wild Space on the planet Agaris. Here, at least a millennia later, they were discovered by cartographers Auric and Rhyssa Graf, who named them Agarians after their adopted home. Agarians have no eyes, so they sense the world through vibrations in the air and through an elevated sense of smell. They grow as vast forests and only need a tiny bit of sunlight to thrive.

Though they traveled to Wild Space to avoid the conflict of the Core Worlds, the Agarians became caught up in the burgeoning Rebellion when the Empire set up a mining colony on their world. The Agarians used their many tricks, including emitting a sleep-inducing gas and explosive seedlings, to attack the Agaris Imperial base and free the Grafs, who had been imprisoned.

I have heard tales of a mysterious mushroom species that can change its shape and size, and can release seedlings as projectiles for use in battle.

PHINDIAN

HOMEWORLD: PHINDAR

Phindians are green-skinned reptilians with long faces and arms. They are extremely cautious and like to stay out of trouble. Osi Sobeck traveled offworld and became the warden of a prison called the Citadel. It was held by the Confederacy for Independent Systems during the Clone Wars, and Sobeck worked for them overseeing their most important detainees. When the Separatists captured a Jedi general, Anakin Skywalker and Obi-Wan Kenobi launched a rescue mission. Sobeck fought them off with help from a droid army but was eventually killed by Skywalker's Padawan, Ahsoka.

THALA-SIREN

HOMEWORLD: UNKNOWN (RECENTLY SEEN ON AHCH-TO)

The docile thala-siren, with its giant flippers, gray-pink skin, elongated neck and snout, and large udders, makes for a curious sight perched atop the rocks, looking out to sea. It is not hunted by the Ahch-To locals, who instead harvest the green milk produced by the female creatures (also known as sea cows) for its nutritional benefits. Jedi legend Luke Skywalker would enjoy a cup of this green beverage while he lived in self-imposed exile on Ahch-To.

As I wandered along the rocky shoreline of this peaceful aquatic planet, I was amused to find myself confronted by a large marine mammal, which appeared to be sunbathing!

MOMONG

HOMEWORLD: WASSKAH

Momongs live on the forest moon of Trandosha and are commonly known as Trandoshan monkeys. They have six limbs, big ears, and long tails, and live high in the trees, preying on birds. Momongs have simple intelligence, proving able to use tools or weapons when necessary.

ARDENNIAN

HOMEWORLD: ARDENNIA

With prehensile toes and four arms, Ardennians are well-suited to military professions, as they are able to be extremely agile and quick in combat. Rio Durant was a good-natured Ardennian pilot who assisted the Republic during the Clone Wars. He later became a smuggler, working with a group led by Tobias Beckett.

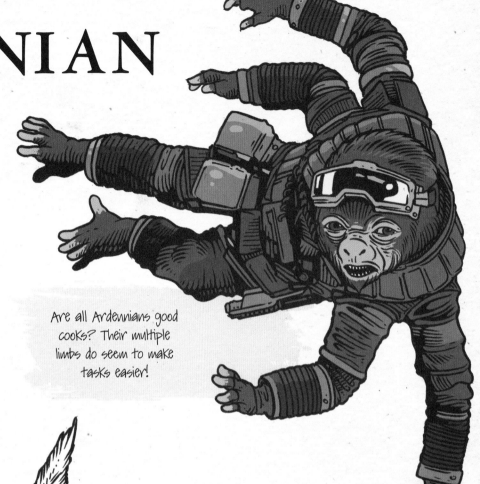

Are all Ardennians good cooks? Their multiple limbs do seem to make tasks easier!

I have heard stories of the abandoned rebel base on the salt-covered planet of Crait. Apparently, the base is home to mysterious foxes with crystal-like fur. These creatures are familiar with all its many passageways, entrances, and exits.

VULPTEX

HOMEWORLD: CRAIT

The vulptices are fox-like in appearance, with keen eyesight that is well accustomed to low light levels, sensitive whiskers that help them navigate darkened areas, and a sharp, crystalline white coat of "fur," which is not only their trademark identifier but also helps act as a defense mechanism against potential predators. A group of vulptices made their home in the abandoned rebel base on Crait.

� text ꓱꓲꓘꓥꓷꓷꓘ

DIANOGA

HOMEWORLD: VODRAN

These strong, seven-tentacled carnivores, also known as garbage squids, feed on refuse and have spread widely throughout the galaxy. They can grow up to a whopping ten meters long. They thrive in dirty water and often board starships when they are docked in port, making their home in the waste tanks. They possess a single eye atop a slimy eyestalk.

I had a most unpleasant encounter this afternoon after delivering some rubbish to the ship's waste compactor. . . .

ꓱꓲꓘꓥꓷꓷꓘ

ARTIODAC

HOMEWORLD: ARTIOD MINOR

Artiodacs are fierce-looking humanoids with huge arms, tough skin, and deep, rumbling voices. They spent centuries enslaved by the Zygerrian Slave Empire, where they were forced to participate in gladiatorial battles in arenas all over the galaxy. This horrible history led to this once quiet and solitary species being thought of as thugs. Many leave their home planet to act as henchmen for crime lords or soldiers in private militias. Strono "Cookie" Tuggs was a disfigured Artiodac chef who worked in Maz Kanata's castle. Though his shocking appearance often held him back in a social environment, Kanata thought of him as a close friend and allowed him to cook for her guests for centuries.

The Mimbanese are known to be experts in camouflage!

MIMBANESE

HOMEWORLD: MIMBAN

This highly aggressive and equally intelligent species hails from a planet so wild and uncivilized that it was ignored for most of its history. The Mimbanese live underground, with vision that is biologically adapted to the low light of their subterranean homes. Despite their lurid red skin, they are skilled in camouflage, covering themselves in mud when facing an enemy. Iasento was the leader of a Mimbanese tribe before the Clone Wars. He and his people were armed and trained by Republic clone troopers to defend their planet from Separatist invaders.

7K↓≡↓K7

RATHTAR

These terrifying beasts are deservedly feared throughout the galaxy. . . .

HOMEWORLD: TWON KETEE

Their role in the infamous Trillia Massacre (during which they killed and ate a large number of beings) has made these huge, slimy, red-skinned creatures extremely sought-after by collectors, who are willing to pay large sums for them. Rathtars are strong, carnivorous, tentacled predators with huge radial mouths full of razor-sharp teeth. They exhibit enough intelligence to hunt in packs. Although they lack a true skeletal structure, rathtars are able to move extremely quickly.

ᚦᚦᚲᚢᚢᚨᚾᚢᚨᚲᚨᚾ

DRAGONSNAKE

HOMEWORLD: DAGOBAH

The dragonsnake is a predatory amphibious reptile that lies in wait below the water for its prey to get close enough before snatching it up with its razor-sharp fangs. Dragonsnakes favor muddy water and swamp areas, which makes them a common hazard on planets like Dagobah, where they can be found hiding in the submerged roots of gnarltrees.

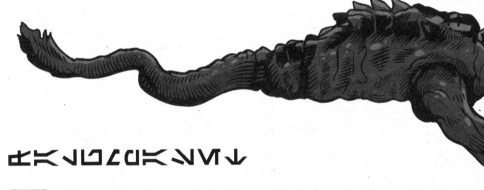

ᚱᚲᚢᚲᚨᚲᚢᚲᚨᚾᛁ

FALUMPASET

HOMEWORLD: NABOO

One of several species to be domesticated by the Gungans, these large mammals performed critical tasks during the Battle of Naboo, such as pulling huge battle wagons. Brown in color with leathery skin, these powerful creatures are herd animals that can be found roaming the plains, forests, and swamps.

The falumpasets are excellent swimmers. The almost disproportionate length of their very long legs to the rest of their body means they can maneuver quickly, which in turn makes them perfectly suited to pulling artillery on the battlefields.

DANZIKAN

HOMEWORLD: DANZIK

Danzikans are a swamp-dwelling species, instantly recognizable by their two heads. Much like the Troigs, both heads are freethinking and they use this to their advantage in card games and business deals. They are often thought of as devious because of their tendency to cheat. Lark and Jonk were nicknamed the twins but forced to participate as a single player at sabacc. Otherwise they would use their double hand as an opportunity to win more credits.

OCTEROID

HOMEWORLD: OCTERO IV

The aquatic Octeroids are known galaxywide for their striking appearance and simple lifestyle. They are gentle giants with little technology, preferring to stay on their watery homeworld. For those who have chosen to explore the galaxy, a breathing apparatus has been developed so they can survive in foreign atmospheres. An Octeroid smuggler known as Big Guy liked to watch games of sabacc. He used to play but found that his singular large eye was reflective and other players could see his cards!

While enjoying a game of sabacc, I was worried about the large, one-eyed alien watching over the game. I assumed he was security, but he seemed to be enjoying himself too much!

SELKATH

HOMEWORLD: MANAAN

Selkath wear chest armor specially designed to house misting vents, keeping their skin moistened. This aquatic species has a reputation for being peaceful. Historically, they have focused on preserving the oceans of their homeworld and caring for the sick. Chata Hyoki and Mantu went against this kind nature by becoming bounty hunters. Hyoki took jobs intimidating senators and participated in the attempted assassination of Padmé Amidala. Mantu was invited by Sith Lord Count Dooku to participate in a competition, where the winner would be awarded the job of kidnapping Supreme Chancellor Sheev Palpatine. Mantu was killed during one of the challenges.

KAMINOAN

HOMEWORLD: KAMINO

The Kaminoans are tall, slender, graceful beings and, as you would expect from expert cloners and master scientists, extremely intelligent. They are a private people who have little interest in the affairs of others, although they are business savvy and will not turn their backs on a money-making enterprise. They travel their planet on graceful aiwhas and have cleverly engineered their stilt cities to be powered by a limitless supply of hydrogen taken directly from the abundance of seawater that covers the planet.

Although it is a long journey (seventy thousand light-years from the Galactic core!) I was honored to take a visit to the great Tipoca city, capital of Kamino, and meet the master scientists who have played such an important part in our galaxy's history.

KARKARODON

HOMEWORLD: KARKARIS

With a long, lean, aquiline build, webbed feet and hands, and a pointed snout, this fearsome species are quick swimmers and have even been known to keep pace with the Republic's military Devilfish submersibles. With no qualms about using their razor-sharp teeth, it's little wonder the Karkarodons had a reputation as fearsome warriors during the Clone Wars.

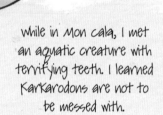

while in Mon Cala, I met an aquatic creature with terrifying teeth. I learned Karkarodons are not to be messed with.

CROCIN

HOMEWORLD: CROCE

Crocins are a reptilian species with short bodies, and teeth that protrude from the tops of their mouths. They build their cities in caverns near water and are unused to bright sunlight. When traveling to warmer climates, they wear protective goggles to prevent damage to their sensitive eyesight. Karjj was an unlucky sabacc player with a bad temper. His love of the game was not diminished by his frequent losses.

PATROLIAN

HOMEWORLD: PATROLIA

This highly intelligent piscine species can be found working in many areas throughout the galaxy. The gills and fins on their heads make them well suited to underwater living, but they are also capable of breathing air and living on the land. They are extremely resourceful and often find work as bounty hunters. When not in the water, their clothes require alteration to accommodate the protruding dorsal fins on their backs.

QUARREN

HOMEWORLD: MON CALA

As a conservative and practical species, Quarren gravitate toward positions of authority. They are a proud but aggressive species and are known to spit ink at their enemies, especially when referred to by the common but derogatory nickname squidhead. Their quick temper previously led them into a civil war with the Mon Calamari.

While enjoying the beautiful aquatic scenery of Mon Cala I observed a disagreement between two of its inhabitants. I recognized the amphibious Quarren from the long growths on its face (hearing organs) and have already encountered them working throughout the galaxy in a variety of jobs, from politicians to accountants.

MON CALAMARI

HOMEWORLD: MON CALA

The Mon Calamari are a common sight throughout the galaxy, often playing a crucial role in galactic events. This aquatic species prefers to live underwater but can survive on land without any special apparatus. Their hatred of the Empire following the occupation of their homeworld led them to become key allies in the Rebellion.

CULTURE

The Mon Calamari are known for being a technologically advanced species with great intelligence and a penchant for art and science. They have also produced many great soldiers and tacticians, using their natural calmness and leadership skills to serve in many galactic conflicts.

Mon Cala is a beautiful aquatic world filled with coral reefs and kelp forests. Mon Cala's capital city is built over a large reef with cruiser-shaped skyscrapers. It is home to two species, the Mon Calamari and the Quarren. They share a monarch and a common language, and have lived peacefully side by side for hundreds of years despite their many differences.

CIVIL WAR

The peace between the Mon Calamari and the Quarren was broken during the Clone Wars when the latter species aligned themselves with the Separatist movement. The Mon Calamari remained loyal to the Republic, and tensions between the two species rose. When the Mon Calamari king, Yos Kolina, died under suspicious circumstances and the Quarren challenged his son Lee-Char's claim to the throne, the two sides prepared for war.

The Jedi and Republic allies stepped in to aid the Mon Calamari but were forced to retreat when the Quarren and Separatist armies attacked with giant, deadly jellyfish. The Mon Calamari were interned in camps, and Lee-Char was forced into hiding. When the Separatist leader Riff Tamson, a ruthless Karkarodon, tried to declare himself the new ruler of Mon Cala, the Quarren had a change of heart. Together, the two species drove the Separatists off Mon Cala, and peace was restored to the planet.

TECHNOLOGY

When they joined the Rebel Alliance, the Mon Calamari brought much-needed support, including a fleet of powerful ships. The Mon Calamari Star Cruisers are huge, with rounded edges, in stark contrast to the dagger-shaped Imperial ships. The cruisers are equipped with turbolasers, ion cannons, tractor beam projectors, and shield generators. These ships provided the Rebellion with an even playing field against the Imperial fleet for the first time since the war began.

MON CALAMARI IN THE GALAXY

General Raddus is heralded as a great rebel hero because he, along with many others, died stealing the plans for the Imperial superweapon, the Death Star. During the Battle of Scarif he led the space assault on the Imperial fleet while Rogue One secured and transmitted the plans from Scarif's surface. Years later, Raddus's name was used for General Leia's Resistance flagship as a tribute to the fallen hero.

Admiral Ackbar was one of the defining characters in the Galactic Civil War, masterminding the rebel attack on the second Death Star at the Battle of Endor. This veteran commander was cool under pressure, a brilliant tactician, and revered by his crew and the whole Alliance.

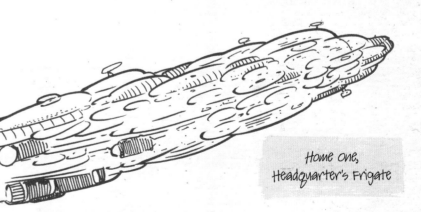

Home One, Headquarter's Frigate

FROZEN LANDS

On my travels I discovered many frozen lands with very few life-forms upon them. But here at the lowest temperatures there were some hardy species that seemed to function, even thrive. I found hairy beasts dwelling underground and in caverns. When I visited Hoth—the site of a famous battle during the Empire's reign—I found the terrifying, predatory wampas, as well as the gentle tauntaun. Even advanced species like the chiss had found a way to make icy planets into homes.

ᛟᚲᚲᛟᚲ

WAMPA

HOMEWORLD: HOTH

These terrifying predators live in ice caves on a remote frozen planet, hunting local prey such as tauntauns. The wampas themselves are seen as great trophies for hunters from all over the galaxy, as they are extremely hard to kill. When Echo Base came to Hoth, wampas were a major concern, as the savage beasts would sneak into the passageways in search of food. When Luke Skywalker was patrolling, a wampa captured him and hung him up in his cave.

ᚢᚲᚱᛟᚲᚲᛚᚣᛖ

NARGLATCH

HOMEWORLD: ORTO PLUTONIA

Narglatches are massive feline beasts with sharp fangs and claws. They are considered sacred by the indigenous Talz, who tame them to use as mounts and hunt them for food. Their pelts are also valuable to hunters. Narglatches are easily felled by modern weaponry. The cubs are so cute that they are kept as pets, but as they grow, so does their ferocity, making them extremely dangerous in confined spaces.

TAUNTAUN

HOMEWORLD: HOTH

Tauntauns are furry, nonsentient creatures well suited to the freezing temperatures of their home planet. They have long claws that allow them to climb icy surfaces and long tails that help them keep their balance while running. Their speed and steadiness make tauntauns excellent mounts for those who can domesticate them. When the rebels established their base on Hoth, they tamed many tauntauns and used them to navigate the icy plains when, due to the cold, their speeders shut down.

shivering and desperate for shelter, I caught a ride across the wastelands of Hoth on a tall, long-necked mount. The smell was terrible, but it navigated the icy terrain in no time.

CHISS

HOMEWORLD: CSILLA

People talk of the great chiss officer, one of the few nonhumans to achieve seniority in the Imperial military. I heard he was ruthless and clever, and not to be messed with.

This mysterious, blue-skinned, red-eyed species is very secretive and largely unknown in the galaxy. The ruling class is made up of royal families called the Aristocra, and they keep little to no contact with the wider universe. Thrawn, a member of the Chiss Ascendancy government, was sent to the Outer Rim to investigate a growing threat and find allies for the Chiss people. Instead of joining his world with the Republic, whom he believed to be weak, Thrawn infiltrated the Empire and rose through the ranks, becoming grand admiral of the Imperial Navy and a favorite of the Emperor.

RUURIAN

While on Lothal I was warned to avoid Ruurians in the marketplace. These curious creatures are renowned pickpockets!

HOMEWORLD: RUURIA

This remarkable species has three evolutionary stages and exhibits advanced intelligence. Eventually they become beautiful winged fliers, but in the first stage they are larva-like creatures full of intelligence and artistic abilities who are actually responsible for running the planet. The second evolution is the pupa stage, where they envelope themselves in self-spun cocoons, to then emerge in the third stage as beautiful chroma-wings. By this stage they have lost much of their early intelligence and are concerned with little but mating and flying. Some Ruurians undergo treatment to stop them reaching this final stage, preferring to hold on to their intelligence instead.

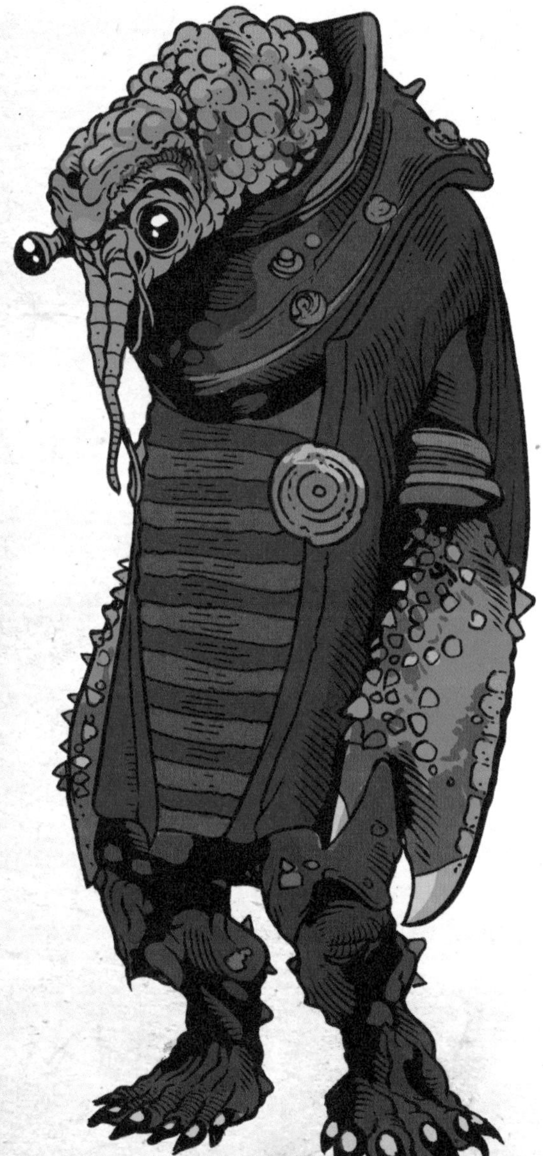

NEPHRAN

HOMEWORLD: NEPOTIS

The Nephran resemble crustaceans, with claws and tentacles on their faces. Not much is known of their history on the water-rich planet of Nepotis. Therm Scissorpunch, a name he likely gave himself, was known to frequent the card tables on Vandor. A particularly sore loser, Therm relied on his fearsome appearance to intimidate his opponents. He had enhanced his fighting prowess with a sharpened shank implanted in his claw.

ᗡ᠊GRINDALID

GRINDALID

HOMEWORLD: UNKNOWN

The Grindalid homeworld has such a dense atmosphere that little light is let in, giving the native species very sensitive eyes that are easily damaged on lighter worlds. Not much else is known about the insect-like Grindalid, but at some point after the fall of the Republic, members of this species formed a criminal gang on Corellia called the White Worms. Most of the gang never came above the surface, but Moloch, a senior henchman, would don protective armor and travel around on land in a truckspeeder.

KOUHUN

HOMEWORLD: INDOUMODO

Although these multilegged arthropods originate from a jungle planet, they can now be found throughout the galaxy owing to their natural ability to adapt to the surrounding environment. Kouhuns can be easily identified by their segmented shells and lethal stingers at the front and rear of their bodies, and their legs allow them to crawl over most surfaces. Their deadliness has made them a favorite weapon among bounty hunters and hired assassins.

If you are unfortunate enough to encounter one of these bug-like creatures at close range, make a calm retreat as quickly as possible! Their venom is HIGHLY dangerous (particularly to humanoid species) and can cause death within mere minutes.

MAZ'S CASTLE

I went to Takodana in search of a famed meeting place for galactic travelers. This lush, green planet is home to a castle filled with spacers and smugglers looking for a haven from the politics and conflicts of the core worlds. This castle is talked about in hushed tones, as those lucky enough to be welcome there do not want to draw the attention of any law enforcement.

The expansive forests, lakes, and grassy plains provided an appealing scene as I flew toward the castle. I landed on the shore of Nymeve Lake and was greeted by a giant statue of the castle's owner, the pirate queen Maz Kanata. The entrance was lined with colorful flags and guests were attended to by a large red droid.

The castle itself was thought to be an ancient battleground for the Jedi and Sith. Despite its age, signs of modern technology were everywhere. I detected sensor grids and communications gear sprouting from the worn battlements, as well as advanced weaponry concealed by many of the inhabitants.

Inside I found a grand hall with lively music and many guests enjoying food and wine. A Bravaisian was peddling her shiny wares while a large Dowutin bragged about his latest hunting trophy. I got the sense many of Maz's guests would not take kindly to my questions, as this was a notorious spot for espionage and underworld activity.

ᗐᑎᒣᑎᗑᑎᘰ

UNKNOWN

HOMEWORLD: UNKNOWN

Like Yoda and Yaddle, Maz Kanata's species was unknown. No other member of this species has ever been discovered, so Maz is believed to have been the only one of her kind. Little is known of her history, other than that she had an extremely long life span, rumored to have lived for over one thousand years.

PIRATE QUEEN

Maz was a small, Force-sensitive humanoid who lived in an ancient castle on Takodana. She allowed travelers into her home as long as they abided by her strict set of rules prohibiting any politics or conflict within the castle's walls. Her guests were provided with food and entertainment, plus supplies for their ongoing journey. All were welcome, including spies, scoundrels, and smugglers. Her home became a refuge for the criminal underworld, and also those who rebelled against the rising powers of the Empire and First Order.

The castle housed many antiques and trinkets that Maz had collected from her travels across the galaxy. She had a strong connection to the Force, despite never becoming a Jedi, and could sense when an object was of great historical value. She somehow came to possess the famous Jedi Luke Skywalker's lightsaber, which he lost in a duel with Darth Vader. Through the Force, Maz could also sense the presence of others and disturbances in the galactic order.

Maz's castle was a permanent home to two droids that aided Maz in enforcing her rules and attended to her guests' needs. ME-8D9, also known as Emmie, was an old protocol droid that served as a translator for pirates and smugglers. She was rumored to have assassin programming and possibly even a history in the Jedi Order. HURID-327 was a large, red load-lifter droid that served as the groundskeeper of the castle.

visiting the vibrant and fascinating fortress on Takodana brought me face-to-face with the oldest living individual I have ever met. I could not get to the origins of Maz's existence. It seemed like she had always been there, welcoming friends to her castle.

HURID-327

ME-8D9
"Emmie"

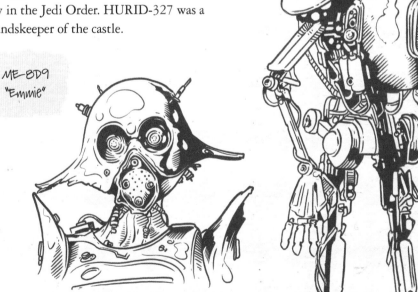

ᗱ7ᛕYᛕ1Ɲ1ᛕᑎ
BRAVAISIAN

HOMEWORLD: BRAVAIS

Bravaisians are a short, long-snouted species with dexterous tongues that they often use instead of their fingers. They are nocturnal, avoiding the intense heat of their homeworld during the day to protect their small, sensitive eyes. Offworld, most Bravaisians wear goggles. Sonsigo and Munduri were podmates who frequented Maz's castle. They were attracted to glittering gems and precious metals, and paid top prices to the sellers. They used their tongues and an electro refractometer to appraise their wares.

Maz's business-minded guests take advantage of the large gathering of customers. I had some treasure evaluated by some keen-eyed Bravaisians.

ᖽᐸᑌ1ᗱ171ᛕᑎ
DELPHIDIAN

HOMEWORLD: DELPHIDIAN CLUSTER

These leathery, stripy-skinned humanoids have a mysterious history. Some believe they were bioengineered as slaves, but the Delphidians themselves never spoke of this. They speak many dialects but rely upon a common language that evolved on Delphidian Cluster to allow for peaceful trade. Sidon Ithano, also known as the Crimson Corsair, was a Delphidian pirate working in the Outer Rim Territories. Though he disguised his identity with a Kaleesh helmet, he was feared by any spacers with valuable cargo. Durteel Haza kept his stripy face on display at Maz's castle.

CULISETTO

HOMEWORLD: UNKNOWN

Culisettos are insectoids that live on blood. They have tubelike mouths, red eyes, and wear traditional brown traveling smocks. A group of Culisettos called the Dengue Sisters spent time at Maz's castle, playing their favorite game of chance, a board game called Deia's Dream.

Grummgar the Dowutin is larger than life in Maz's castle.

DOWUTIN

HOMEWORLD: DOWUT

Dowutins are large, combative humanoids known across the galaxy for producing fierce mercenaries and hunters. They are aggressive-looking, with chin horns, sharp claws, and thick skin. Dowutins are forced to fend for themselves from a young age and must quickly learn hunting skills to survive. Grummgar was a famed game hunter and often sold his services as a gun for hire. When he wasn't illegally poaching animals from distant worlds, he spent his time at Maz's castle gathering hunting tips from fellow explorers.

HASSK

HOMEWORLD: HASSKYN

The Hassks are a hairy, aggressive species of subhumanoids. They are almost completely covered in fur, except for their hairless, gray-skinned faces filled with terrifying fangs. They have sensitive hearing and keen night vision, all the better for hunting. Hassks are near-feral and are thought of by most as wild animals. They live in a very primitive culture with limited technology. When they were first confronted with space travel, many left their homes and sought out worlds to wreak havoc, particularly in places of ill repute. The Hassk triplets were thugs who spent time at Maz Kanata's castle stirring up trouble. Led by Varmik, the triplets engaged in skirmishes with their battered VT-33d and DH-17 blaster pistols but were often thwarted by Kanata's more powerful patrons.

A furry yellow character offered to change my face—how rude!

FRIGOSIAN

HOMEWORLD: TANSYL 5

Frigosians are a small, clever species with dome-shaped heads and are covered in yellow fur. They have large mouths with sharp teeth, and their eyes are so sensitive they have to wear protective goggles on certain planets. The atmosphere on some planets is so different from Tansyl 5 that Frigosians have to wear breathing apparatus to survive. Thromba and Laparo were cryptosurgeons who worked on Takodana offering cosmetic procedures to patrons of Maz's castle. They were very popular with spacers and smugglers who needed to disappear.

UBDURIAN

HOMEWORLD: NAG UBDUR AND UBDURIA

Ubdurians are bald, sentient humanoids with dark eyes and no visible nose. They often wear traditional traveling smocks with aurodium belt buckles. Prashee and Cratinus were Ubdurian brothers who were often found gambling at Maz's establishment. As identical twins, they would often play tricks by swapping identities and carrying out profitable scams on their fellow travelers.

A purple creature sat quietly in the corner. His elongated trunk was a fascinating facial feature I don't believe I've ever seen before. . . .

ONODONE

HOMEWORLD: UNKNOWN

Onodones are easily recognizable by their trunk-like mouths that are so long they can be draped over their shoulders and looped around. They are rarely seen and often missing from galactic events, so not much is known about this unusual species, their history, or their homeworld. Gwellis Bagnoro was one such enigma, who spent a great deal of time at Maz Kanata's castle on Takodana. Kanata's guests were sure to be asked no questions, and Bagnoro was particularly secretive about his past as an expert forger. Some Onodones have shorter snouts, as seen on a patron in Maz's castle.

NABOO

In the Mid Rim region of the galaxy is the planet of Naboo, covered in swamps, lakes, rolling plains, and mountains, and populated by a vast variety of species. The tall grasslands are perfect for concealing small predators on the hunt, as well as providing food for grazing herd animals.

The royal city of Theed is renowned for its culture and artistic pursuits, with many universities, religious buildings, and tourist attractions. I was drawn to the elegant architecture, especially that of the Royal Palace with its domed roofs and clifftop vista.

I took a submarine to explore the underwater world of Otoh Gunga, home of the native Gungans. In contrast to the peaceful animals aboveground, the swampy lakes of Naboo were filled with menacing creatures. A giant fish with terrifying teeth knocked into me, and I had to avoid crustaceans as big as starships! The amazing sight of a plasma city under Lake Paonga was worth the effort.

ꓷꓲꓳꓷꓵꓱꓭ

PIKOBI

HOMEWORLD: NABOO

These remarkably fast-moving, flightless reptavians can be found on Coruscant and Onderon as well as their homeworld of Naboo. They are highly agile little predators perfectly suited to swampy and steamy jungle environs. With long beaks for hunting and spearing prey, and webbed feet, they move quickly on both land and in water. Remarkably, they have the ability to shed their tails when necessary. This long tail helps them balance when on land and it appears they can cast it off when under attack! They are able to then regrow it at a later stage.

ꓷꛂꓵꓲꓳꓳꓭ

PELIKKI

HOMEWORLD: NABOO

These river-dwelling birds, closely related to ducks, have a notably large bill, which helps them hunt their prey. They also have a marvelous throat pouch, which expands to hold their catch. These birds remain largely untamed, although in some areas the human inhabitants of the planet feed them for pleasure.

ꓥꓷꓥꓗ

NUNA

HOMEWORLD: NABOO

Although these omnivorous, two-legged, flightless birds are native to the swamps of Naboo, they have spread across the galaxy and can commonly be found on Tatooine and Saleucami as well. They are not intelligent creatures, but they are easy to care for and have become prized for their meat and eggs. Just one bird can feed an entire family of four! The nuna also has the accolade of being the only animal to be used as a ball, in the widely played game of Nuna-ball.

ᚠᚲᛚᚴᚴ
FAMBAA

HOMEWORLD: NABOO

Of the three native creatures to be trained
for combat, the fambaa is the largest. As
with their fellow falumpasets, fambaas are a
common sight on the battlefields of Naboo,
supporting the Gungan Grand Army and often
operating in tandem to carry shield generator
equipment and booma cannons. These massive
creatures are primarily domesticated as beasts
of burden and artillery draft beasts. Offworld
(particularly in Abafar), their meat is served as
a delicacy in a dish named Fambaa Delight!

ᚾᛖᚲᚲᚷ
SHAAK

HOMEWORLD: NABOO

Shaak are gentle, friendly animals, raised for their meat. They leisurely
graze on the grasslands, traveling in herds. There are many stories of
shaaks losing their footing and slipping into the numerous rivers that
traverse Naboo, but thankfully their blubber makes them extremely
buoyant—allowing them to simply float along until they reach
land!

It's hard to believe these
mighty "swamp lizards"
roaming the plains in
front of me actually
hatch from eggs!

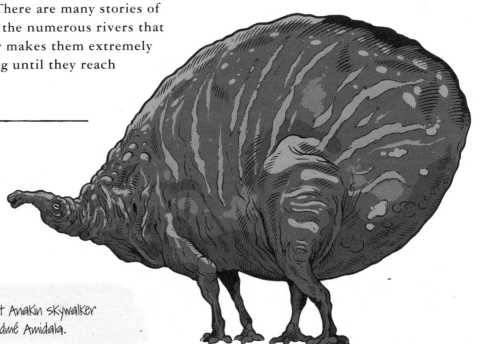

I could not help laughing when I first saw this
strange, bulbous creature. It is very plump but has
only four small, weak legs in contrast. It is so out of
proportion that it often struggles to stay upright!

shepherds who frequent the lake country tell me that Anakin skywalker
once tried (badly) to ride a shaak, to impress Padmé Amidala.

KAADU

HOMEWORLD: NABOO

These two-legged, duck-billed reptavians live mainly on land but can also breathe underwater. Despite being wingless, these swamp dwellers are agile and extremely swift animals thanks to their long legs. Sharp hearing, an excellent sense of smell, and an aptitude for endurance, combined with loyalty, add to their list of credentials as the perfect mount. Domesticated kaadu could often be seen sprinting into battle with Gungan calvary commanders, like the famed Jar Jar Binks, on their backs. They must have been quite a sight, decorated with giant, elaborate tail feathers!

MOTT

HOMEWORLD: NABOO

This horn-nosed, striped herbivore is a favorite pet among Gungans. Living in herds of up to fifteen animals, they eat swamp vegetation and are adept at foraging for food in the undergrowth using their nose horns. Unfortunately, their small size makes them an easy target and primary food source for many other predators on Naboo. However, as they have a high reproduction rate of about fifteen calves to a litter, they have happily never been in danger of extinction.

SLUG-BEETLE

HOMEWORLD: NABOO AND TATOOINE

The roots of the perlote tree, found only in these swamps, are home to this small insect that is drawn to both desert and damp conditions. Slug-beetles are considered a delicacy by the Gungan inhabitants of Naboo, who are able to eat the insect whole. Senator Jar Jar Binks, famous warrior of the Clone Wars, is particularly partial to them.

As I carefully picked my way through the Eastern swamps of Naboo, a small, winged beetle of the most beautiful blue caught my eye.

GUNGANS

HOMEWORLD: NABOO

Gungans are tall, amphibious humanoids with large lungs suitable for holding their breath underwater, long tongues ideal for scooping up small prey from the Naboo swamps, and strong legs adapted for swimming. They live in underwater cities far removed from the politics and culture of the human Naboo population aboveground.

CULTURE

The city of Otoh Gunga is made up of bubble-like structures designed to keep water out but allow Gungans to pass through. These structures hold around a million residents and are anchored to the lake floor by stone pillars. The Gungan population is not governed by the Naboo royal leaders but in a clan-based system led by a chief and the Gungan High Council. This chief is called a boss and can make military and law enforcement decisions for the whole species.

Gungans are a proud warrior species, and each city has its own army to protect its people. These armies come together during times of war to form the Gungan Grand Army. With their warrior mentality and advanced weaponry, this is not a force to be messed with. Gungans often use land-based animals for work that cannot be done underwater. They farm shaak for meat and use their skins for clothing. Falumpasets are employed to pull carts and small cargo, whereas fambaa are used for transporting heavier items, such as shield generators. They can also be used to carry weapons on the battlefield. Gungan warriors ride kaadu, as they are quick and sturdy.

GUNGANS IN THE GALAXY

Jar Jar Binks played a key role in galactic events when he was thrust into the complicated world of Coruscant politics. This clumsy but well-meaning Gungan became a liaison between Queen Amidala and the Gungans, and helped bring about an alliance between the two in the war against the Trade Federation. He went on to become a senior representative for Naboo in the Galactic Senate, but corrupt politicians abused his trusting nature, and he unwittingly participated in allowing the Emperor to come to power.

WEAPONS AND TECHNOLOGY

Though many people elsewhere in the galaxy mistake them as primitive, Gungans are actually fairly technologically advanced. They have developed the materials that make their cities so functional, as well as formidable weapons for their warriors. Gungan energy balls, which they call boomas, come in various sizes and can be fired from catapults, slings, or by hand. They pack a punch against advancing land-based enemies. Personal energy shields are carried by each warrior on the front line and are designed to protect the user against blaster fire and physical weapons. They can also be expanded to cover complete troops to protect against airborne attacks.

The manta-shaped hull of the bongo submarine perfectly fits with the underwater population, while tentacle-like fins spin to provide powerful acceleration.

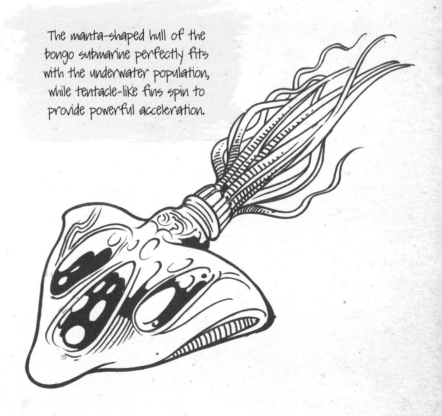

There's always a bigger fish. . . .

SCALEFISH

HOMEWORLD: NABOO

The waters of Naboo are teeming with these small, colorful fish, and they can particularly be seen in Lake Paonga around the city of Otoh Gunga, to which it is believed they are attracted because of the numerous glowing lights. Seven varieties make up the scalefish species: doos, rays, mees, faas, sees, laas, and tees. A valuable food source to both humans and Gungans, they are considered harmless, with the exception of the faa, which is carnivorous, and the mee, which has a poisonous spine.

I was offered a trip to the underwater tunnels but declined, having heard tales of the fearsome-looking creature known to attack Gungan submersibles.

OPEE SEA KILLER

HOMEWORLD: NABOO

The opee is a curious creature, exhibiting the shell-like armor and limbs of a crustacean while still possessing piscine characteristics. It inhabits the deep abyss, clinging to rocky outreaches until it can lure prey close enough with its long antennae. The opee is then able to swiftly give chase using a unique jet propulsion movement, sucking water in through its vast mouth and expelling it through small vents at the back of its body. Once in striking range, it uses its long, sticky tongue to grab its prey and drag it toward its doom.

COLO CLAW FISH

This fearsome deepwater predator is the stuff of nightmares!

HOMEWORLD: NABOO

The colo can be found haunting the underwater tunnels close to the core of the planet. Its tail is studded with bioluminescent markings to attract prey, and its forelegs hold terrifying claws. As well as a row of razor-sharp teeth, this carnivorous creature possesses venomous fangs that it uses to stun its prey once caught. With distending jaws and an expanding stomach, the colo is able to devour prey bigger than its own head! However, colos must ensure their prey is dead before ingesting it. Their digestive systems are slow, and they run the risk of being eaten from inside out if the prey remains alive. Despite their fearsome appearance, the colo is considered by the affluent to be an edible delicacy.

SANDO AQUA MONSTER

HOMEWORLD: NABOO

Having heard of this mysterious creature, I must confess that I believed it to be a terrifying myth.

Although the sando aqua monster is rarely seen in the wild, the large carcasses of these creatures have occasionally washed up on the beaches of Naboo, proving this mysterious creature is undeniably real. The biggest of the predators on Naboo, the sando needs to feed constantly. It has webbed claws and a long, powerful tail that propels it through the water. It has razor-sharp teeth and a mouth so wide it can consume most other creatures in just one bite. Sando aqua monsters are thought to be extremely protective of their young.

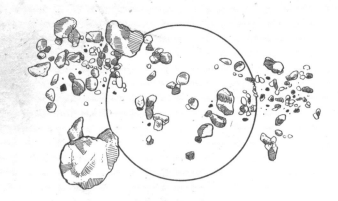

ᚲᚢᚾᚱᚲᚢ ᚲᚢᚾ ᚢᚲᚢᚾᚢ

AERIAL AND SPACE

Having traveled across many planets and experienced varying landscapes and climates, I have always marveled at the species that occupy the skies. From the high-flying birds of prey to the peculiar winged mammals used as mounts, the aerial population of this galaxy are often some of the most colorful and curious creatures discovered on my journey.

On my way between planets, when not in hyperspace, I have come across strange and sometimes frightening space-dwelling aliens—mostly by accident. These creatures inhabit the bleakest parts of the universe and are often savage in nature.

ᛞᛖᚱᚾᚢᚢᛁᛇ ᛖᚱᚾᚾᚱ

WHISPER BIRD

HOMEWORLD: YAVIN 4

Famed for their beautiful golden plumage, these amazing birds are able to fly noiselessly, giving rise to their apt name. They have a trademark low-pitched call but are able to employ their ability for silence when hunting. Their diet in the wild consists of fish and weeds. Although native to the moon of Yavin 4, they have also been introduced on Coruscant and Null.

ᚺᚩᚾᚤᚩᚱ CONVOR

HOMEWORLD: VARIOUS, BUT INCLUDES ATOLLON, MALACHOR, AND WASSKAH

With their highly attractive brown-and-gold plumage, these small birds are popular pets throughout the galaxy and their beautiful feathers can often be seen on display in luxury garments. Although attractive and elegant, they are also cunning when it comes to protecting themselves from would-be predators. Possessing a prehensile tail, convorees are known to work in pairs to pick up an attacker, lift it into the air, and drop it from a great height. This is very common in the jungles of Wasskah, where they are hunted by the aggressive momong. On Wasskah, the convorees live in spiny brambles.

convorees have the most beautiful golden feathers.

ᚢᚩᚱᚷ PORG

HOMEWORLD: AHCH-TO

The little porgs are evolved from the same stock as Lanais, but without the intelligence of their sentient neighbors. However, they are entertaining creatures that dive into the sea to catch fish for their young (known as porglets). They have a flat nose, forward-facing eyes (which make it easier to spot fish), webbed feet for swimming, and dense feathers for insulation, and are also known to be talented mimics. They are very curious about any new arrivals on their home planet. When Chewbacca landed on Ahch-To, he considered porgs a tasty treat but found it hard to kill the winged creatures when the pack turned their sad eyes on him.

I've heard tales of the dramatic clifftops of Ahch-To, covered in the most curious small birds.

K10ΞK

AIWHA

HOMEWORLD: KAMINO

On Kamino, I took an exhilarating ride on an aiwha—a flying whale!

These massive creatures are certainly unusual, being native to both the waters and sky of Kamino thanks to wing-fins that can effortlessly take them from the ocean depths to the skies above. It is rumored that the Kaminoans genetically modified the aiwhas to be suitable for the harsh Kamino environment. Their amazing physiology uses a water vascular system that allows them to control their own density—absorbing water into spongy tissue to increase weight when beneath the waves, then releasing that weight in preparation for flight. Their notable long beaks contain a sieve that allows them to filter plankton in both the air and water.

ЗΔⴱ◻1Λⴱ

BOGWING

HOMEWORLD: NABOO

These flying reptavians are extremely strong and have been known to carry up to nine times their own weight. Bogwings are used in a favorite Gungan pastime called gulliball. They fly on to signal the interval halfway through the game.

ᗷᖇᕮᘔᗩᛕ

BREZAK

HOMEWORLD: ZYGERRIA

The brezak is surprisingly graceful as it carries the Zygerrian elite through the sky.

Also known as the Zygerrian gliding lizard, this large reptavian has the impressive ability to fly. It doesn't have wings, but it does have large skin flaps connected to its ribcage that it is able to spread wide. Once fully extended, these flaps allow the brezak to glide on air currents. It is further aided by its light bone structure and flat tail, which can be used as a steering device, much like a ship's rudder. On Zygerria, the royal family use domesticated brezaks as mounts for both themselves and the palace guards.

DACTILLION

HOMEWORLD: UTAPAU

These large winged creatures are carnivorous reptiles that the native Utai have successfully domesticated by feeding them meat (previously, they themselves would have been on the dinner menu). These powerful fliers are an important means of transportation on Utapau, being able to traverse great distances quickly. While they live in sinkholes, the dactillion are able to ride thermal updrafts into the air using their wings, then scramble up rocky ledges using their claws. They are also valuable mounts in battle, able to grasp enemies with their strong claws, and the two prominent pronged horns at the ends of their beaks can be used in both defense and combat.

CARRIER BUTTERFLY

HOMEWORLD: MARIDUN

These attractive little insects hide a surprising secret—the ability to
recognize and repeat instructions. This amazing skill led to them being
used to carry messages to allies during the Clone Wars. The Lurmen
colonists kept the tiny creatures as pets, but also used them as a way of
communicating messages and warnings. The butterflies were able to listen to
the instructions of their owners, then fly to the desired recipient and repeat
the message. They were an extremely important tool during this time, as it
was almost impossible to catch one of these tiny creatures in the wild.

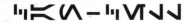

CAN-CELL

HOMEWORLD: VARIOUS, BUT INCLUDES KASHYYYK, RODIA, AND TETH

No mere insect, this impressive species of flying insectoid possesses capabilities that belie its odd
appearance. With two large green eyes, six legs, and a long, segmented tail, these creatures are a particular
favorite among Wookiees, who believe them to be bringers of luck. As such, they're often kept as pets
by Wookiees and even inspired the design of many of their vehicles. Oddly, can-cells are attracted to
the buzzing sound these vehicles make and can often be found in abundance at landing sites. They can
be domesticated and make brave mounts for those small enough to ride them. Both Yoda and Anakin
Skywalker have ridden can-cells in their time.

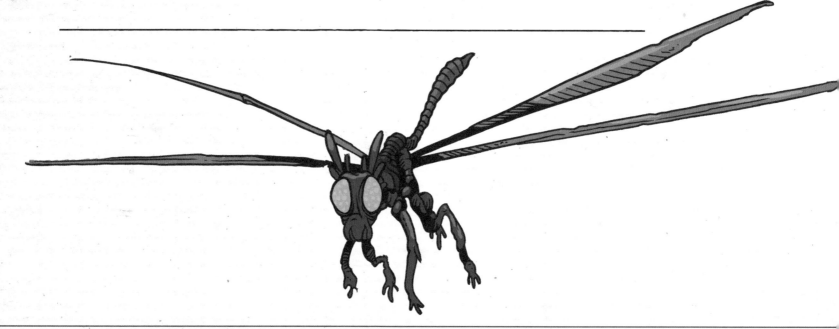

TIBIDEE

HOMEWORLD: STYGEON PRIME

The bleak and desolate frozen world of Stygeon Prime is home to these huge, curious creatures often loathed by starship pilots. Although normally gentle and not prone to attack unless threatened, tibidees are able to detect different frequencies and can mistake them for a mating call—which can be problematic for a ship's crew. Apart from this, they are graceful creatures who fly through the air thanks to a combination of giant, flat wings and internal gas bags. With the exception of the inmates of the notorious prison known as the Spire, tibidees are thought to be the sole inhabitants of Stygeon Prime.

A flash of color across the bleak landscape caught my eye as tibidees flocked across the sky.

XANDU

HOMEWORLD: IEGO

These tan-colored, flying predators possess four strong, leathery wings, fangs, two arms, and two legs with claws. They also have huge ears that they use to listen out for potential prey—even at great distances. Xandu are territorial creatures and very strong, able to carry the weight of a human. The xandu has a nasty—but effective—habit of snatching up its prey in its claws, then smashing it against a rock wall.

As I was climbing the great rocky spires of this planet, I became aware of a shadow overhead. Looking up, I saw a six-eyed creature flying above me. It was a xandu.

EXOGORTH

Forget myth and legend . . . these goliath space slugs truly are a sight to behold!

HOMEWORLD: VARIOUS, BUT INCLUDES THE HOTH ASTEROID BELT

Often found living in asteroid fields, exogorths burrow deep within rocks. As silicon-based life-forms they feed on the minerals and stellar energy emissions that naturally occur around asteroids, as well as mynocks and even hapless starships and their crews who have mistaken an open mouth for a simple cave. These giant slugs have sharp teeth and sensory organs and reproduce by splitting in two. They are able to push themselves away from their current asteroid and float through space to land on another—miraculously surviving the vacuum. These giants of the cosmos can grow to a massive nine hundred meters.

PURRGIL

HOMEWORLD: DEEP SPACE

Amazingly, purrgil are able to naturally travel in hyperspace after consuming enough of the gas Clouzon-36. In fact, legend cites these creatures as the inspiration for our current hyperdrive technology. Unfortunately, they often materialize from hyperspace in the paths of starships, causing terrible accidents. As a result, many spacefarers now fire at these creatures on sight. This is sad; when floating majestically through the stars, they are certainly a sight to behold.

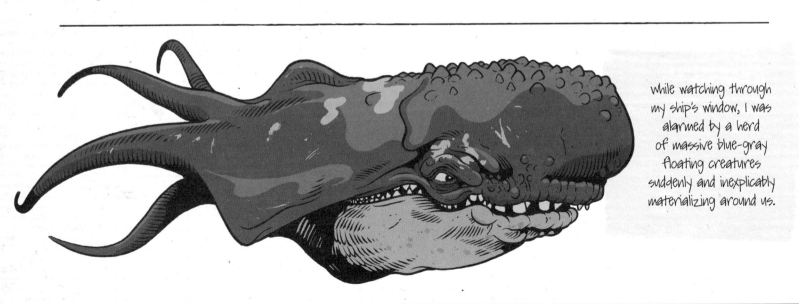

While watching through my ship's window, I was alarmed by a herd of massive blue-gray floating creatures suddenly and inexplicably materializing around us.

FYRNOCK

HOMEWORLD: ASTEROIDS

The ferocious fyrnocks are hostile, four-legged predators that possess sharp teeth and claws, a long tail, and glowing yellow eyes. As with other silicon-based life-forms, the fyrnocks thrive on thin-atmosphere asteroids, feeding mainly on small space slugs and mynocks and the plethora of naturally occurring minerals and rocks. Interestingly, they are unable to hunt in sunlight and must instead limit their attacks to the cover of darkness.

MYNOCK

HOMEWORLD: MAINLY DEEP SPACE, ALTHOUGH A FEW VARIETIES INHABIT PLANETS

This silicon-based, parasitic species is loathed almost universally throughout the galaxy. Found in deep space, they are drawn to energy and are often sighted clinging to starships, draining the craft's power supply. They also inhabit mineral-rich asteroids and have been known to survive in the dark, damp stomachs of exogorths for years before finally being digested. Despite this, in some quadrants mynocks are hunted for their meat. They can be edible when prepared correctly.

NEEBRAY MANTAS

HOMEWORLD: TATOOINE

These huge, limbless flying creatures soar through the skies feeding on stellar gasses and, despite usually being peaceful, can become violent toward ships when provoked or threatened. After birth, the Neebray infants live among the coral forests of Rugosa, which serve as a relatively safe nursery environment until adulthood. The largest recorded wingspan of a Neebray is 1,674 meters.

DOMESTICATED CREATURES

I have found throughout the galaxy that highly intelligent species often domesticate less-advanced animals as pets. These creatures often have little practical purpose but are kept for comfort and entertainment, and even sometimes as a sign of the owner's wealth and status. Some of them are Kind of cute, I suppose.

↓◌◌ᒷ ᒲᐯᗑ ᒷ◌ᐯᒷ-ᔕᒲᐯ↓

TOOKA AND LOTH-CAT

HOMEWORLD: FOUND THROUGHOUT THE GALAXY

These fuzzy felines are predominantly employed in starship holds to hunt vermin and keep the ship pest free, but they are also affectionate, friendly little creatures. Sharing many similarities with Loth-cats, tookas are a common sight throughout the galaxy and come in a wide variety of colors, from purple to yellow, with a flat face, small nostrils, and two beady, dark eyes. They have a large mouth (which apparently contains twenty-eight long, pointy teeth!) and sharp claws that they use for both catching prey and climbing. While they mainly eat vermin, they also enjoy nuna and milk. Loth-cats frequently inhabit the Lothal prairie grasslands, which are not only home to their Loth-rat prey but also afford them cover for hunting. Loth-cats can be temperamental in the wild but loyal companions once domesticated.

A tooka

A Loth-cat

BARGHEST

HOMEWORLD: UNKNOWN

Barghests make excellent pets for those who require protection. Their sharp teeth and six red eyes scare enemies away, and though aggressive in nature, they are extremely loyal to their owners. At Maz's castle, Gwellis Bagnoro was never seen without his pet barghest, Izby.

PUFFER PIG

HOMEWORLD: UNKNOWN

Although they are funny-looking little things with plump bodies and wide-set eyes, puffer pigs are actually extremely valuable. They have a superior sense of smell that is attuned to locating precious minerals. When these strange creatures are threatened, they puff up to three times their usual size, giving them their name. Mineral mining was restricted during the reign of the Galactic Empire, so these odd-looking pigs became hugely popular on the black market.

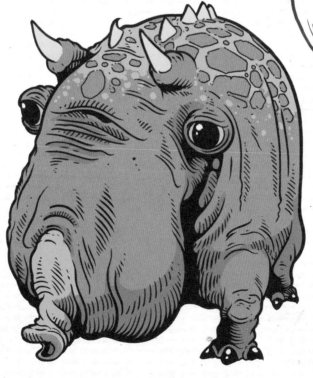

A commotion in the marketplace caused a fright to a strange little creature, who reacted by blowing up like a balloon!

CORELLIAN HOUNDS

HOMEWORLD: CORELLIA

Across Corellia, there is a wide variety of quick and nimble canines used by the locals for a number of tasks. Due to their keen sense of smell, they are often bred for hunting and tracking. They have a vicious bark and bite, so they can be quite effective for protection. Criminal gangs are also fond of using these hounds for defense or to attack their rivals. Sibians are a particularly popular breed, as they have regenerating teeth, a sturdy set of scales on their heads, and can be harnessed for use in combat.

corellian-hound tamers are crazy. Even with their padded clothing and protective gloves, they are still in biting range of those terrible teeth!

It seems I am too tall to ride a fathier, but they are wonderful to watch.

FATHIER

HOMEWORLD: UNKNOWN

Fathiers are majestic creatures used as mounts and on affluent worlds for sport. They have long legs, are extremely fast, and are easily domesticated. On Canto Bight fathiers are raced by jockeys, and spectators can bet on the outcome for entertainment. These creatures are often exploited due to their natural compliance and the great sums of money that can be made through gambling on the races. Fathier jockeys take their lives in their hands, as a fall during a race is almost always fatal, but the career is very appealing due to the fame and fortune it guarantees.

ᒋᐊᓚ˙ ᐯᐃᒋ

KOD'YOK

HOMEWORLD: VANDOR

Kod'yoks are peaceful herd animals that roam the open plains on the snowy planet of Vandor. The locals use them for transportation, but they are also farmed for their meat and milk. Their hair is useful for creating the hard-wearing clothing necessary for surviving the harsh climate.

ᓭᓚᐃᐧᓚᓚᐧᐯ

BLURRG

HOMEWORLD: RYLOTH AND ENDOR

The mighty blurrg is extremely versatile, and although not intelligent, this two-legged reptilian species is highly prized for its strength, speed, and determination. These fascinating creatures walk on their two hind legs and possess a huge mouth, which is capable of chewing through almost anything. This led to them being used to great effect in agriculture, where farmers employ blurrgs to clear grass and weeds and haul equipment. However, when provoked they can become vicious and were even employed as mounts to fight against Separatist troops during the Clone Wars. Clone troopers and Twi'lek guerrillas rode the speedy creatures into battle, as they could reportedly match the velocity of Imperial speeder bikes!

Blurrgs are very useful. I think they can carry almost anything!

149

DEJARIK

Dejarik is a popular game in which a player competes by moving holographic pieces across a board in a bid to defeat their opponent's pieces through combat. The pieces are based on creatures I have not come across, and most are believed to be mythical monsters, but who knows. . . .

MOLATOR

A magical creature from an Alderaanian myth, this piece is oddly given the name Grimtaash.

MANTELLIAN SAVRIP

Large creature from Ord Mantell.

HOUJIX

Rumored to be a popular pet on Kinyen.

MONNOK

A primitive hunter from a desert world.

K'LOR'SLUG

Possibly a swamp dweller from the Outer Rim.

NG'OK

Unknown origins, but a likely predator due to its deadly claws.

KINTAN STRIDER

A ferocious creature from the planet Kintan.

GHHHK

Believed to be a tree dweller from the planet Bith.

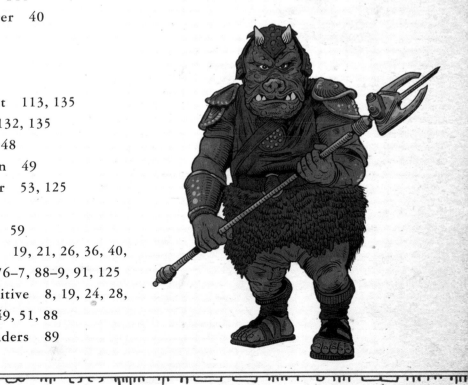

U

V

W

X

Y

Z